"Stay here with me," the stranger whispered, his voice rough with weariness. *"Just until I'm asleep."*

"It's all right," Sarah murmured. "I won't leave."

But even when he was asleep, she didn't pull away.

How would it feel to bend and kiss those lips? she wondered. To have him open his mouth beneath hers? Open those beautiful eyes and gaze at her with surprise and pleasure?

The thought made her take a long, shuddering breath.

It would be so easy to fall into his arms. He would welcome her—she'd seen that much in his eyes. But for how long? Until tomorrow? Until someone came to arrest him—or kill him?

She had to step back. She had to remember that this was a stranger who'd come into her life only because he needed her help.

A forbidden stranger—and one far too dangerous for any woman's peace of mind....

Dear Reader,

We've got some great reading for you this month, but I'll bet you already knew that. Suzanne Carey is back with *Whose Baby?* The title already tells you that a custody battle is at the heart of this story, but it's Suzanne's name that guarantees all the emotional intensity you want to find between the covers.

Maggie Shayne's *The Littlest Cowboy* launches a new miniseries this month, THE TEXAS BRAND. These rough, tough, ranchin' Texans will win your heart, just as Sheriff Garrett Brand wins the hearts of lovely Chelsea Brennan and her tiny nephew. If you like mysterious and somewhat spooky goings-on, you'll love Marcia Evanick's *His Chosen Bride*, a marriage-of-convenience story with a paranormal twist. Clara Wimberly's hero in *You Must Remember This* is a mysterious stranger—mysterious even to himself, because his memory is gone and he has no idea who he is or what has brought him to Sarah James's door. One thing's for certain, though: it's love that keeps him there. In *Undercover Husband*, Leann Harris creates a heroine who thinks she's a widow, then finds out she might not be when a handsome—and somehow familiar—stranger walks through her door. Finally, I know you'll love *Prince Joe*, the hero of Suzanne Brockmann's new book, part of her TALL, DARK AND DANGEROUS miniseries. This is a royal impostor story, with a rough-around-the-edges hero who suddenly has to wear the crown.

Don't miss a single one of these exciting books, and come back next month for more of the best romance around—only in Silhouette Intimate Moments.

Yours,

Leslie Wainger

Leslie Wainger
Senior Editor and Editorial Coordinator

Please address questions and book requests to:
Silhouette Reader Service
U.S.: 3010 Walden Ave., P.O. Box 1325, Buffalo, NY 14269
Canadian: P.O. Box 609, Fort Erie, Ont. L2A 5X3

YOU MUST REMEMBER THIS

CLARA WIMBERLY

Published by Silhouette Books

America's Publisher of Contemporary Romance

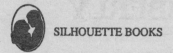

SILHOUETTE BOOKS

ISBN 0-373-07718-1

YOU MUST REMEMBER THIS

Copyright © 1996 by Clara Wimberly

This edition published by arrangement with Harlequin Books S.A.

® and TM are trademarks of Harlequin Books S.A., used under license. Trademarks indicated with ® are registered in the United States Patent and Trademark Office, the Canadian Trade Marks Office and in other countries.

Printed in U.S.A.

Books by Clara Wimberly

Silhouette Intimate Moments

Ryan Blake's Revenge #521
Georgia on My Mind #612
You Must Remember This #718

CLARA WIMBERLY

writes her novels in a one-room cabin in the woods, built for her by her husband and two sons. She loves American history and traveling to old settlements and villages, where she says she finds a lot of wonderful ideas and inspiration. "I suppose if I have been influenced by anything, it is the South and the area where I live," Clara says. "In the mountains there are hundreds of quaint stories and unusual characters."

To my friend Jane McIlwain,
a lady who has it all:
intellect, charm and an outrageous
sense of humor that's kept me laughing
for more than twenty years.

Chapter 1

Sarah James muttered beneath her breath as she struggled to drive through the pouring rain. The blacktopped county road leading back to the farmhouse was narrow and poorly marked. The lines had faded to a bare visibility and she had to squint to see well enough to keep her pickup truck on the pavement.

She hadn't known when she left earlier that it would storm so badly or she might not have gone. But her friend Lacy had insisted, pleading with her to get out of the small farmhouse if only for a little while.

"I understand your need to be alone, Sarah," Lacy had said. "But you have to start living again. It's been more than a year. There won't be anyone here except you and me. No one to see the scar or ask any questions. We'll have a nice quiet dinner together—the way we used to do. How about it? I'll make my famous Georgia Pine Bark Stew and Peanut Butter Pie."

"Bribery," Sarah had said, laughing aloud. It seemed like forever since she'd laughed.

The accident that took away her laughter had happened a little over a year ago. Ironically, she and her husband, Joe, had gone out to celebrate the news that they were going to have their first child. It had been a stormy, rainy night much like tonight. But they had barely noticed the weather.

That night as they drove, Sarah had continued talking and laughing even when a truck pulled up swiftly behind them and flashed its lights. How vividly she could still recall the look of surprise on Joe's face. He had glanced up into the rearview mirror, his face clearly illuminated by the lights behind them.

"Wild kids," he'd muttered, laughing.

Then slowly she saw the laughter leave his eyes. Two small lines appeared at the bridge of his nose and then his gaze shifted nervously toward Sarah.

"Joe? What is it?" she'd asked.

"More of my imagination, I'm afraid."

She'd known immediately what he meant. The case he'd been working on as a television journalist had taken up most of his time lately.

The story was so big, so complicated that sometimes he wouldn't even bother to explain it to her when he came home tired and weary. But she knew it involved survivalist groups. Men who spent their weekends in the woods, armed to the teeth and fully convinced they would be called on at any time to defend their homes. Some of them sold illegal guns and military equipment stolen from various army bases; others dealt in drugs. Joe even suspected that there were ties to elected county officials.

All Joe's imagination, the sheriff had told him.

"Drop it, Joe," Sheriff Metcalf had said. "Before you get your fool self killed and leave that pretty wife of yours a young widow."

Sarah's husband had been very upset when he came home from that meeting.

"I wouldn't be surprised if the sheriff were involved in this, too," he'd said.

"No," Sarah had whispered, staring at his troubled face. Her grandfather had known Sheriff Metcalf all his life. He'd voted for him the year before he died.

"Maybe I'm wrong," Joe said. "But something about this is just not right."

Joe had pretended to heed the sheriff's words, backing off his demand that the group be investigated. But it hadn't stopped him from continuing his undercover investigative work on the story. He'd often been angry and frustrated that there was no help from county law enforcement.

Just before the accident they had begun to receive hate messages on their answering machine. Hang-up calls in the middle of the night. Chilling warnings that Joe should check beneath his car before starting it in the mornings.

Joe had even installed a burglar system on the car only to find the wires disconnected a day or two later.

Sarah envisioned how Joe had tried to speed away from the truck that night. "Hold on, honey," he'd said, clenching his jaws together.

She closed her eyes, remembering. It had happened on a road similar to this one. Isolated and straight. Closed in on both sides by towering pines glistening with rain when the headlights touched them.

Suddenly the vehicle behind had bumped them. Sarah screamed and reached for Joe.

"Joe!" she screamed. "Your seat belt. You didn't fasten your seat belt!"

She was the worrier and Joe was the daredevil. He often teased her about that. But how many times in her life had she warned him...cajoled him into fastening his belt? She'd even tried to frighten him with stories of accident victims brought into the emergency room. But he had thought himself invincible. And that night, she knew he fully expected he could outrun the truck.

Their small car slid sideways on the road, but Joe had managed to regain control. In the dashlights, she saw the muscles in his thigh flex as he pushed the gas pedal all the way to the floor.

Sarah had felt the speed in every inch of her body, making her heart accelerate, making her breath come in small gasps as she clasped her hands together and whispered silent prayers.

The truck behind caught them easily and rammed them again, then pulled around until their hood was even with the car's rear fender.

What happened next was a nightmare that still woke Sarah in the middle of the night, drenched in sweat. How many times since then had she lain awake for hours with the same horrible, dark feeling of impending death. Even now, just remembering the feeling made her heart beat faster.

The truck had slammed into them, pushing the small car around sideways on the slick road. She remembered the horrible feeling of sliding out of control, the sound of gravel crunching beneath the wheels and Joe's curses as he struggled with the wheel. Then there was the surreal feeling as the tires caught and the car began to flip. Over and over...

"Joooe!"

Sarah gripped the wheel of the truck and shook her head, trying to shake away the last thing she remembered about that night—the sound of her own voice calling out her husband's name.

Why on earth had she let herself remember any of it? Especially while driving on a night like this.

She shook the memories away. She had become too thoughtful and introverted since the accident. Lacy had been telling her that for months. Especially after Sarah insisted on remaining in the country even after she had recovered from her injuries.

It might have been different...*she* might have been different if she hadn't lost the baby, too, a few days after the wreck. If she'd had something to live for, something to look forward to in those first dark months after Joe's death.

Sarah shivered and tried to concentrate on the road and her driving.

Squinting through the darkness and rain, she thought she saw lights ahead and her hands automatically tightened on the steering wheel. For some reason she felt a little tingle of alarm race down her arms.

Much of the countryside from Wayland to the ocean was farmland. The Colonial Coast, as the tourist brochures called it. Miles and miles of cultivated fields, or cattle pasture. The rest of the swampy countryside was piny woods—thousands of acres of flat country and tall, slender pine trees. A great deal of it belonged to the federal government or the state of Georgia, but no one bothered with it except when it was necessary to fight an occasional forest fire.

Funny that the very thing that frightened her now about being out here in her grandparents' old home—the isolation and quiet—was one of the things that had appealed most to Sarah at first. After Joe's death, and with the terrible scar on her face, Sarah had wanted to be as far away from people and traffic as she could. It was the one thing she thought might save her sanity.

"It's a car," she muttered, focusing again on the lights ahead of her. Peering through the rain-spattered windshield she saw two definite spots of light. Was the vehicle stopped? Was it an accident or...?

She heard something then. A muffled explosion, like the spat of a gun. But was it a gunshot, or just her heightened imagination? She told herself it was probably nothing more than a car backfiring.

Suddenly the carlights coming toward her brightened. She could sense that the vehicle was moving now and she breathed a quiet sigh of relief. Even with her nurse's training, she wasn't sure she was ready to assist with a car accident.

A dark van sped past her, heading toward town. It was going too fast, at an almost frenzied speed, she thought.

Sarah found herself trembling as she watched the glimmer of red taillights in her rearview mirror and saw them disappear into the rainy darkness. Without realizing it, she had slowed her truck to a crawl. There were no other lights for miles now, either ahead or behind her. She could hear her own unsteady breathing mingled with the quiet thump of the windshield wipers and the loud hiss of rain on the cab of the pickup.

"For heaven's sake," she muttered, shivering. "Get a grip."

She had thought too much about what happened last year, that was why she was so unsettled. Tonight, in the downpour, everything had reminded her. And it was not a good time to be out driving, or remembering.

Instinctively Sarah reached up to touch the raised red line on her face that ran from the corner of her mouth almost up to her hairline. It was an ugly scar. But one that could be repaired, the surgeons had assured her, whenever she was ready.

But she wasn't ready. Simply because she didn't care. Joe's death had devastated her and she was still bitter that she didn't even have his child to help soothe the ache in her heart. She wasn't sure she would ever care about anything again. At this point, she thought she might be content to stay hidden away in the country forever, at least until the insurance money ran out. And that could take a long, long time.

"It's all right," she whispered to herself.

In a few minutes she'd be in the warm, dry safety of the house. What she'd seen was nothing. Probably just a van full of teenagers playing their usual Saturday night pranks.

Sarah thought she'd never been so relieved to see anything as the sight of the reflectors that marked the driveway to the farmhouse.

She allowed herself only a moment of panic when she pulled into the driveway and noticed that the security light in the yard was out. So were the other lights she'd left on inside the house.

She put the truck into Park and grabbed a flashlight from the seat. Then, pulling her jacket over her head, she made a dash through the rain to the porch.

Sarah felt a tingle of apprehension race up her back. The hair at the back of her neck prickled and she turned to wave the light out through the rain and over the soaked bushes and thicket beyond the yard.

"Is anyone there?" she called. "Tom?"

Was that silly cat out there in the bushes somewhere? She hadn't really heard anything to make her think that. It was just a feeling, a heart-pounding anxiety that she couldn't quite explain. Almost as if someone were watching her.

"Tom . . . is that you?" she called again.

Finally she waved the light toward the end of the porch. The big gray striped cat, hearing her call, had crawled out of his warm, cozy box and stretched now before padding slowly and silently across the wooden planks toward her.

Sarah smiled and bent to scratch his furry head. When she straightened and unlocked the door, her hands were trembling.

She held the door open for a minute, wishing that for once, the stray tabby who had wandered here a few months ago, would finally come inside.

"Want to come in?" she asked softly . . . hopefully.

Tom rubbed against her legs, then sniffed the cool air that drifted out of the house. But in the end, he turned and sauntered back toward his box on the porch.

Sarah hurried inside, feeling somewhat safer once she closed the door and was standing in familiar territory. God, was she turning into one of those people who never ventured out into public? Who had panic attacks unless they were in the security of their own home?

She muttered irritably as she flicked a switch and confirmed that the storm had knocked the electricity out. Flashing the light around the darkened house, she assured herself that nothing was amiss and that the place was just as she'd left it a few hours earlier.

In minutes she had candles glowing in the hallway and bathroom, and in her bedroom across from it. And at the end of the hallway, the light from a kerosene lamp in the kitchen spilled warmly out across the wood floors.

Sarah hung her wet jacket on the hooks of an antique hall tree and went into the bathroom to dry her hair. It was then she heard the sound, quiet and muffled.

The thump of a car door? A limb falling on the roof? Or had it been a footstep on the front porch?

Sarah swallowed hard and picked up the flashlight again. If she'd learned anything from living out here alone, it was to face her fears immediately. Waiting and thinking only heightened her phobias.

She walked to the front door and pushed back the curtains that covered the small window at eye level. She pressed the flashlight against the glass and what she saw made her heart seem to stop.

A man stood there in the darkness, slumped over slightly, his shoulder pressed against one of the porch posts. Lightning flashed and outlined him for a moment like some eerie scene from a movie.

Sarah wanted to scream, to run. But to her horror, not a sound emerged from her lips. Her feet, instead of moving, seemed cemented to the spot.

She couldn't see his face. In fact, he didn't even appear to be looking toward the house, but seemed intent on keeping himself upright.

He's hurt, her nurse's voice cried. Help him!

And yet her trembling hand did not move toward the door's lock.

Suddenly she turned and ran to the phone that sat on a table in the hallway.

The line was dead.

Slowly she went back to the door, hoping that what she'd seen was a vision. Her imagination. That somehow the stranger would be gone.

Instead she saw him lying on the porch, his legs hanging down over the steps into the rain.

This time she didn't think. She reacted with instinct and compassion, opening the door without hesitation and hurrying to the fallen man.

Raking the light over him, she murmured quietly when she saw the pool of blood beneath his head.

"My God," she whispered, falling to her knees on the porch beside him.

This was not a victim of a car accident. His hands were tied behind his back and the blood on the porch came from a head wound that looked serious.

When she touched him, his skin was wet and cold and she could feel him shivering beneath her hands. Quickly she searched for a pulse in his neck. It was weak, but it was there and she whispered a silent thanks that he was breathing. But Sarah knew he might already be in shock from the cold and from whatever terrible fate he had met out there in the gloom and rain.

Sarah's eyes lifted and scanned the darkness past the porch. She saw nothing; heard nothing unusual. The sound of rain and thunder blotted out everything else.

She gripped the man's jacket, and turned him onto his back. He groaned, but still didn't open his eyes.

"It's all right," she whispered, wiping the rain and dirt from his face. "You're safe now...you're all right. Just hold on...do you hear me?"

He was not a big man, but his shoulders were broad and she could feel the corded muscles beneath his clothes. Still, it was a struggle to drag him inch by inch across the porch toward the door. Stories she'd heard crossed her mind, about the effects of fear and adrenaline on a person's strength. It was the only way she could account for the fact that she was able to pull him into the house and the front bedroom.

She found a pair of scissors and cut the plastic ties that bound his hands and dug into his wrists. Freed of restraint, his arms fell limply onto the floor.

By the time Sarah had dragged and pulled him up onto the bed, every muscle in her body screamed from the effort. Finally, her task accomplished, she fell back onto the floor, exhausted and panting for breath. She could feel her heart pounding and she was aware of her cold, muddy clothes sticking to her body.

She stared at the man on her grandparents' old iron bed. If he had been unconscious this long he might be gravely wounded. She might not be able to give him the help he needed. After all, it had been a year since she'd practiced nursing.

Finally she managed to drag herself up from the floor and run into the hall to try the phone again. Hoping desperately that the line might miraculously have cleared, she listened carefully. But there was still no dial tone.

"Oh, no," she murmured. Sarah pushed her wet hair away from her face and went back into the bedroom to stand looking helplessly at the wounded man.

"You'll have to do it, Sarah James," she told herself. "There's no one else. So don't just stand here—get busy."

Quickly she ran through the house to find more candles and a kerosene lamp. She couldn't spare any more time thinking or wishing there were some other way to help this man. She had to stop the bleeding and see how serious his condition was.

She kicked her wet shoes off as she hurried back and forth from the kitchen to the bedroom, bringing warm water, towels and bandages along with a lamp and candles.

She could hear his breathing. It sounded quiet and shallow and every now and then it would catch in his throat and he would groan and mutter words she couldn't understand.

Sarah put the lamp beside the bed and went to work, first cutting and pushing away his jacket and shirt to see if there were other wounds besides the one on the side of his head.

His skin was battered and bruised but there were no wounds to his chest.

"Thank you, God," she whispered. Her eyes moved over his bare skin, from the steadily beating pulse at his throat, to the thick mat of dark hair on his chest. He was well built and though the smoothness of his hands indicated a lack of physical labor, he looked like a man who kept himself in top condition.

Hesitating only a moment, she unbuckled his belt, feeling a little uncertain as her knuckles brushed against his flat stomach.

She averted her eyes as she cut away his wet underwear and then pulled a quilt up to cover his naked body. He wasn't the first man she'd seen that way, she reminded herself.

As she began to work at cleaning his face and chest, her attention was immediately distracted by his strong, handsome features. Straight brown hair, cut close on the sides, spiked over his forehead. And even as wet and muddied as he was, she caught the faint scent of an expensive men's cologne.

His brows were dark and finely shaped and long thick lashes lay against his skin. His nose, straight and narrow, made Sarah think of an old-world aristocrat—haughty and well cared for, a man used to the best.

It took only minutes for Sarah to determine that his head wound was a graze, deep, but not life threatening. But the look of it troubled her. Somewhere in the back of her mind she'd seen wounds like this before. And if she were not mistaken, it was caused by a bullet. She could think of no other explanation for the long, straight groove that missed killing him by mere centimeters.

And the fact that he was still unconscious worried her, too.

She applied antiseptic to the wound and placed a bandage around his head and then another around his chest. She couldn't be sure without X rays if he had cracked ribs, but the bruising was certainly bad enough to indicate they might be.

Just when she finished taping the bandage, the man on the bed moved and muttered something beneath his breath. Sarah knelt beside the bed, very close to him.

"Can you hear me?" she asked.

He didn't answer or open his eyes.

The dim light in the room couldn't hide the fact that he was very handsome. Beautiful even. And Sarah found herself wondering absurdly what color his eyes were. She wished they weren't hidden from her beneath those still, closed lashes.

She touched the scar on her cheek rather self-consciously and continued watching him for any sign that he might be waking up.

His head moved restlessly back and forth on the pillow. He seemed troubled as his hand reached out toward Sarah.

She flinched when his fingers grasped her wet shirt.

"Don't...don't..." he murmured.

He seemed to become more agitated and desperate and Sarah was surprised at the strength of the hands that grasped her shirt and dragged her toward him. She moved up onto the bed, sitting beside him and taking his wrists in her hands in an effort to quiet him. She could feel the raw, ugly marks that the plastic strips had left on his dark skin.

Whoever he was, his pain and desperation were real and that was something Sarah couldn't ignore. She found her old compassion returning, that nurses's instinct of wishing she could do more to help him.

She also felt an odd urge to soothe his scraped, bruised skin. She frowned at her reaction, although she knew it wasn't so unusual for a nurse to have such sympathy for a patient.

She just wasn't so sure that was what this feeling was. But no matter who the man was, or what he'd done, she told herself, he was her patient now and he was entirely dependent on her for help.

She let her fingers linger on his wrist, touching his damaged skin as her other hand reached out to his forehead to brush the damp hair away from his eyes. His skin felt cold and he moved his head back and forth against the pillow. His eyes were closed tightly and he was frowning.

"I'm going to help you," Sarah whispered. "Shh, I'm here. I won't let anyone hurt you again."

Even in his unconscious state, her words seemed to calm him, yet his hands still moved restlessly, clutching, pulling at her as if he needed to tell her something.

"Cord . . ." he whispered. "Get . . . Cord." A thin sheen of perspiration appeared on his forehead as he seemed to struggle with some inner demon.

What was he trying to tell her? It was obvious that he was in danger, but who was this person named Cord? Someone who could help him . . . or the man who'd tried to kill him?

She shivered as she sat watching his troubled expression, unable to help. She knew she probably should get up and change out of her own wet clothes. But she was so curious about this man and she wanted to know what had happened to him.

Why had someone tried to kill him? For all she knew he could be a criminal, although she was certain he wasn't an escaped convict, not dressed the way he was.

Finally, when he didn't move or try to talk again, she left the bed and went to gather up his wet, muddied jacket and shirt that she'd tossed on the floor. She pushed the material of the shirt back and read the label in the back.

"Charvet," she murmured. Not a name she was familiar with, but looking at the material and French cuffs, obviously an expensive one. The label in the tie was also unfamiliar. *"Tino Cosma?* Sounds rich," she murmured.

She tossed the shirt and tie across the back of a chair and concentrated on the double-breasted jacket of the suit. Sarah thought it was probably the most elegant piece of work she'd ever seen. Certainly nothing anyone she knew could afford. Not even the doctors at their hospital dressed this well.

The small discreet label read *Zeidler and Zeidler.* "Private Collection," she read.

She turned to look at the man on the bed, then back at the suit in her hands.

He could be a high-rolling drug dealer for all she knew. Involved perhaps in a drug deal that went bad. There were rumors in the small farming community about low-flying vintage B-52's that roared over the countryside in the middle of the night. Some residents swore they'd even seen packages dropped from the planes into isolated pastures, or deep in the swamp.

Others whispered about the possibility of a gun-running trade that operated from the coast near Brunswick and right through Ware County, then over to the Interstate and up into Atlanta.

The same rumors Joe had been investigating when he died. But since his death no one had come forward to take up the case.

There was no telling what kind of business this man was involved in. And despite her compassion for him, Sarah warned herself that just because he was handsome and well dressed, it didn't mean he wasn't dangerous . . . or a criminal.

But there was no denying the fact that he had been the victim tonight, and that he needed her help desperately. At least now that she'd carefully examined him, she knew he wouldn't die. She could safely wait until morning to notify the authorities. Surely the phone would be working by then and the man would be awake.

Sarah's eyes raked over him, from his dark hair, down his bare chest to where she'd pulled a quilt up over the lower part of his body.

She didn't know him, knew absolutely nothing about him. But she'd be willing to bet he wasn't a Southerner. More likely he was from New York or Chicago.

"For heaven's sake," she chided herself. "That hardly makes him a criminal." She sounded like her friend Lacy who didn't trust any man living north of the Mason-Dixon line. Sarah laughed softly remembering some of Lacy's eccentric ideas.

Sarah paced the small room as she continued to watch the man on the bed. It was possible that whoever had done this might come back looking for him. To make sure he was dead.

Her gaze turned toward the windows. She didn't think she had heard another vehicle pass since she came home. Could the van she saw speeding back toward town have been involved in what happened to him? Could the sound she'd heard on the road have been the gunshot that had caused this wound to his head?

Her hand reached up to cover her mouth and her eyes. When her gaze rested again on the stranger, it was troubled and filled with apprehension.

Her appearance on the scene tonight could have interrupted something. After all, the man was bound and helpless—if they'd meant to kill him, why hadn't they? Unless they saw her lights and panicked, giving this man a chance to run.

What if someone came back, looking for him... intending to make certain he was dead now that no one was around to see. Would they see that her house was the only one in the area...see the truck they'd passed on the road parked in her driveway and put two and two together?

Or was she becoming completely paranoid from living out here alone for so long?

As crazy and farfetched as her fears sounded, she knew she couldn't take a chance. To be on the safe side, she could at least move the truck to the garage until morning.

Quickly she ran into the hallway and grabbed her raincoat from the hall tree. Outside on the porch she picked up a broom leaning against the house. She held the broom out into the rain to wet it and then scrubbed away the blood from the wood floor.

She felt something rub against her legs and she jumped.

"Oh my Lord, Tom," she whispered. "You're going to scare me to death yet." She reached down and ran her fingers along his soft furry coat. "You're very wise to stay here out of the rain."

Sarah had never been a cat lover. But when this old tomcat had wandered, scraggly and thin from hunger, onto her porch one morning, she had fed him and brushed the burrs from his striped fur. He hadn't been too friendly and when she sent him on his way, she'd never expected to see him again.

But he'd come back. At first he'd show up every few weeks, later only a couple of days would go by between his appearances. Gradually he began to trust her and to stay longer until finally he just decided to make the place his home.

He hadn't demanded much attention. He was as independent as she was and he absolutely hated being cooped up in the house. He preferred prowling the yard or barn and the fields that lay between the house and swamp. His independence suited both of them well, but he was good company and Sarah had grown used to having him around.

"Scat," she said. "I've got to move this truck and I'm sure you don't want to go out in the rain and ruin your beautiful fur. Go back to bed." She smiled as he meowed and continued pacing the porch while she ran out into the rain.

She drove the truck into a garage that was several yards from the house, then locked the doors. Back inside the house she peeked in on the wounded man before going to her bedroom next door to change into dry clothes.

When she came back to his room, it was late. Sarah was so exhausted she knew she'd never be able to stay awake for the rest of the night. But she needed to be here, in case he woke up.

What if he woke and became violent for some crazy unexplained reason? After all, she didn't know him or what kind of man he was. She didn't know anything about him. And she certainly didn't relish the idea of trying to sleep with those disturbing possibilities in the back of her mind.

"It's unlikely he'll do anything," she told herself, shaking her head and staring at him.

But her imagination was working overtime after all that had happened. And she had to admit she was more than a little nervous about having a mysterious stranger, wounded or not, in her house while she slept.

She bit her lower lip as an idea came to her. Then she went to a nearby dresser and rummaged through the drawers. She took a deep breath and stared with misgiving at the old nylon stocking that she held in her hands.

She'd only tie his ankles and arms loosely to the bed. Just so she could feel safe while she slept. Until she could find out who he was and why someone had left him for dead on a lonely Georgia road in the middle of the night.

Sarah quickly set to her task, tying the gossamer nylons around the man's ankles and then to the foot of the iron bed. Carefully she placed his arms down by his sides, wincing as she tied the nylons loosely to his scraped wrists and then to the bed frame beneath the mattress.

She stood back, still feeling unsure about what she'd done. He wasn't the first patient she'd helped restrain, usually for the patient's own good. But if this man weren't dangerous or a criminal, he'd think she was some kind of nut when he woke and found himself tied to the bed.

Hopefully in the morning she'd learn that he was completely harmless. Then someone would come and take the man to the hospital in Wayland where he could be properly cared for. He wouldn't be her responsibility any longer.

She'd go about her business of gathering wildflowers for her watercolor paintings and working in her small herb garden out back.

She'd be alone again.

Just the way she wanted it.

Chapter 2

When Hagan opened his eyes, sometime before dawn, he grunted slightly and closed them against the dizzying ringing in his head. He took several deep breaths before slowly opening his eyes the second time. Without turning his aching head, he let his gaze move slowly around the room.

At first he saw the woman out of the corner of his eye and he thought he must be dreaming. She was a small, fragile-looking creature curled up in a rocking chair a few feet from the bed. Her head rested against her arm and a mass of dark hair tumbled down over her face.

Hagan blinked, wondering why the light in the room was so dim. Then he noticed the half-melted candles and the glimmer of light through an old blackened lamp globe.

Where in hell was he? As he continued looking around the rather old-fashioned room, he felt as if he had been catapulted back into the past, to some strange time he'd never been before.

He was aware of a throbbing ache in his side, which hardly compared to his terrible pounding headache. He could barely make himself move his head enough to see the neat white bandage that wound around his rib cage.

What the hell had happened to him?

He remembered the rain. The sting of it on his face as he struggled through wet brush and soggy grass. He remembered the scent of grass and rich earthy soil and from somewhere the sweet lingering smell of wild wet roses.

Hagan closed his eyes tightly and tried to turn over to alleviate some of the pain in his side. But something held him down; he couldn't move. When he realized that something was tied around his wrists, he opened his eyes and frowned. His disbelieving gaze moved toward his right arm, which felt numb. He could hardly believe it when he saw the reason. He was tied with some thin material to the bed. Then he realized his spread-eagled feet were similarly tied to the foot of the bed.

"What the hell?" he muttered.

He jerked his arm against the restraint and began to curse. And even though his movements caused the pain in his head to become even more excruciating, he continued kicking his feet against the bindings.

He turned his head suddenly toward the sleeping woman and saw that she had come awake. Her face was turned slightly away from him and was in shadow, but she was looking at him fearfully, as if he were the very devil come to life.

Why the hell should she be afraid? He was the one tied up like a Christmas turkey.

"Please," Sarah whispered. She stood up and lifted her hand toward him, but she didn't move any closer to the bed. "Don't do that. I'm afraid you'll hurt yourself."

Hagan grunted humorlessly and gritted his teeth.

"Hurt myself?" he said, his tone incredulous. "Darlin', I believe someone has already beat me to that," he replied sarcastically. "You didn't happen to get the license number of the truck that hit me did you?"

The first thing Sarah noticed, besides his deep voice, was that it carried the soft, rolling accent of the South. And that surprised her. She'd been so certain he was what Lacy referred to as a transplanted Yankee.

"I...I was afraid you'd try to get up while I was asleep," she said, lying. "That you might injure yourself." Now that the man was awake and staring at her with those angry, glittering eyes, she didn't have the nerve to tell him that she'd tied him to the bed because she was afraid of him.

She still was. Seeing those furious eyes made her even more fearful than before.

"Look," Sarah said. "Why don't you just tell me who you are and what happened, then I'll..."

The man frowned and shook his head. There was an odd, confused expression on his face as his eyes moved quickly over the room and then down at his own body.

"What the hell's going on here?" he muttered. A sheen of perspiration glistened on his forehead and his skin had turned very pale.

"Are you all right?" Sarah asked. She moved toward the bed. "Are you in pain or—"

It was his eyes that stopped her. Those cold, dark eyes that pinned her to the floor and kept her from coming any closer.

"What did you give me...did you drug me? What the devil's going on?" His voice cracked and Sarah could hear panic in its depths.

"I...I didn't give you anything...of course I didn't drug you."

He seemed genuinely confused and alarmed as he glared at her. Was his problem mental? Was he some paranoid patient who had escaped from a hospital?

"Just tell me your name," she said, trying to keep her voice soft and nonthreatening.

"I..." He frowned again and shook his head. His mouth opened as if to speak, but no words came out.

"That's the problem," he finally managed to say. "My God. I don't know...I don't know my own name." He looked up at her and swallowed hard.

Sarah bit her lip, staring at him for a moment. But she believed him. The desperation and confusion on his face could not be faked. Besides, as a nurse, she knew that short-term amnesia was not uncommon with a head wound, not to mention the trauma he'd obviously experienced last night.

His gruff voice dragged her attention back to reality.

"Untie me," he demanded. In one split second his expression changed from one of confusion to anger. "Cut these...these damn things..." The muscles in his arms strained against the nylons as he pulled, only making them tighter.

"Don't..." she said, reaching out.

"Look sugar," he growled. "I don't know what game you're playing here or who the hell you think you are, but I want out of here. And I want out now."

Sarah stood very still. She did feel sympathy for him. She even believed he was telling the truth. But she wasn't about to untie him...not after seeing that dark look of fury in his eyes.

"Am I not making myself clear?" he snapped. He strained against the ties until the entire bed shook. "Where are the others? Tell your boss man I want to see him. Agh..."

He gasped as a pain shot from his ribs all the way to the top of his head. It forced him to close his eyes and lean his head back against the pillow. As his body tensed from the pain he took a long, deep breath of air.

"Please . . . calm down," Sarah said. "You're making absolutely no sense. I think you probably have amnesia . . . from the wound to your head. But I have no idea who this boss man is you want to see."

"Oh, that's cute," he said. "I'll have to give you credit, baby, you have this sweet innocent act down pat."

"What?" Sarah asked, blinking against his sarcastic accusations.

"Look," he said, his voice hard with impatience. "Someone had to carry me in here. Do you really expect me to believe you did that all by yourself?" His eyes raked over her petite figure.

"I can't help what you believe or what you don't believe," Sarah said. She hardly knew what to think of the man and his strange accusations. Was he delirious? "But that's exactly what happened. I dragged you in here myself."

"Yeah, right."

Hagan stared at the woman in the wavering light of the lamp. Her actions were suspicious even now. After all, she *had* tied him up. And she seemed very careful to stay out of his reach in case he broke away from his bindings. She kept her face turned slightly away from him, just out of the small circle of light that the lamp made, as if she didn't want him to be able to identify her later.

"Untie me," he said, cursing again and pulling against his restraints.

"I . . . I can't do that," she said.

Sarah didn't know what to do. Doubts swirled around in her head. The man was wounded and obviously in great pain. But he was surprisingly strong and more than a little determined. The thought of keeping him tied, of keeping *anyone* tied was repulsive to her. She didn't even like the idea of keeping a bird or animal caged or bound. But there was a look about him—a wild-eyed look of danger that frightened her and warned her not to let him loose so quickly.

"Now, dammit," he said, the words coming like a growl from deep in his chest.

"Listen to me," Sarah said. She crossed her arms over her chest, almost protectively, and took one step backward, away from the intensity of his eyes. Those eyes that were still hidden in the shadows of the dim room.

"I'm a nurse and this is where I live. There was a very bad storm last night and the lights and phone are still out. You came to my porch, wounded and bleeding, with your hands tied behind your back."

The man frowned and glanced down at his wrists where the red marks from the plastic ties were still visible.

"I had no idea who you were, but I tried to help you as best I could. Still, I'd be a fool to go to sleep with a man in my house that I don't know, a man someone tried to kill. Now I'm sorry if you're uncomfortable, but—"

"Uncomfortable?" he growled. He was staring at her as if she were the crazy one. "Uncomfortable, lady, is hardly the word I'd use to describe how I'm feeling at this moment."

"You won't have to stay here much longer," she said, shaken by the intensity of his anger. She thought she'd never met a man with such raw fury, as if it were just waiting to explode.

"Really?" he drawled, his voice caustic. "What are you waiting for—the marines?"

"Your sarcasm is not going to make me trust you any quicker," she said quietly. "As soon as the phone is back on, I'll call the sheriff and—"

"No," he said, moving restlessly as if he might lunge at her. "No sheriff," he said, shaking his head. "And no doctors."

Hagan shook his head. He didn't know where it came from, but some deep, gut-wrenching intuition told him not to trust anyone. Not the sheriff. Not even a doctor.

Sarah signed with exasperation.

"Why?" she asked, her eyes narrowing with suspicion.

"I don't know why." He chewed at his lower lip and seemed lost in thought. "Intuition," he said, shrugging his shoulders. "At the moment it's all I have. All I can do is ask you to trust me."

Sarah laughed, a quick noise of disbelief.

"Trust you?" she asked.

"I guess you'd be a fool to trust a stranger who wandered into your house in the middle of the night," he said. He wished he could see her better. That she would step closer to the bed so he could see her eyes.

"Yes, I certainly would," she agreed.

"And you're not a fool," he said, his voice growing quiet.

Sarah turned her head to one side as she caught a different tone in his voice. She watched him as if he were a snake, getting ready to strike.

What was it in his voice? A hint of flirtatiousness . . . a seductive flattery?

Charm, she decided. Plain, old-fashioned Southern charm. Calculated to win her over, if she weren't mistaken. But charm it was, and it seemed to come quite easily to this man.

"But I do know one thing about you," he continued.

"What's that?" she asked, still cautious.

"If you were willing to call the sheriff to help me, then you probably aren't involved with any of the people who tried to kill me."

"I told you I'm not."

"You have to remember," he said with an arch of his brow. "I don't know you any better than you know me."

Sarah nodded slowly. "That's true."

"But tell the truth," he said. "Could I really have been lucky enough to wander into the home of a *nurse?* And one who lives out in the middle of God knows where?" He glanced with curiosity around the room.

"I swear I'm a nurse," she said. Without realizing it, her hand moved up to touch the scar on her face, still hidden in the shadows from the man on the bed. "Although to be perfectly honest, I haven't practiced nursing for over a year. That's why I'd feel much better if you'd at least let me call a doctor . . ."

"And safer?" he asked, his eyes glinting at her.

"And safer," she admitted.

"Sorry, honey . . . no doctors."

Sarah shivered at the flinty dismissal in his voice. He might not know who he was, but he certainly seemed to know what he wanted. "Maybe I should point out that you're hardly in a position to be making any kind of demands," she said, openly challenging him, despite the way her insides trembled.

He grew very still and his gaze reached across the room to confront her.

"You can't stay awake forever," he said, his voice quiet . . . deadly.

Sarah shivered. Something in his eyes frightened her. But she met his gaze, determined not to back down from his challenge.

"Someone tried to kill you," she said. "I did the best I could, but you have this memory loss, which could be a sign of something even more serious. I wish you'd just let me—"

"I said no."

Hagan stared at the woman through narrowed eyes, trying to decide if she was lying, and if she really was what she said. Slowly he let his gaze wander around the room, taking in the faded wallpaper and old furniture.

She didn't belong here, he was sure of that.

But where did she belong? She'd said it was where she lived, but somehow the pieces didn't all seem to fit where she was concerned. If this wasn't her home, then whose was it and why was she here alone?

"What's your name?" he asked, turning his gaze back to her. He noticed how pale her skin was and now that his eyes had focused somewhat he could see that her dark hair held glints of auburn in the dim light. She was small and fragile and quite beautiful from what little he could see.

But it was her eyes that captured his attention. They were big and expressive and seemed to be a very pale color—blue or green, he couldn't tell. They were fringed with dark, thick lashes and in the depths of those eyes, Hagan thought he'd never seen such sadness. And he wondered why.

"My name is Sarah James," she said without hesitating.

"Sarah," he said, his voice deep and low.

Sarah blushed.

There it was again, that hint of something in his voice. That charming hint of quiet intimacy that made her feel jumpy and self-conscious. As if he'd touched her. As if he knew her and could actually see into her thoughts.

"Well, Sarah James," he said, his voice still holding that odd caressing tone. "I can't help noticing that someone has undressed me." Hagan glanced with wry amusement down at his bare chest and stomach. "That would have been you, I presume . . . since we're all alone here."

"I . . . yes," she said, lifting her chin and meeting his rather mocking gaze. "Of course it was me. You were wet. Your clothes were wet and . . . after all, I am a nurse," she added with exasperation.

"You don't have to explain," he said, still mocking her. "But since you refuse to cut me loose, I suppose you'll just have to help me with a few things." His steady look was devilish.

Sarah looked puzzled.

"The bathroom?" he said with a knowing lift of his brows.

"Oh. Oh . . . yes . . . of course."

He had managed to catch her completely off balance and for the life of her she didn't know what to say. Or what to do.

She put her hands to her burning cheeks. She couldn't understand why he made her feel so unfocused and embarrassed. She had helped male patients with every intimate bodily function imaginable. At this point there wasn't much about the male anatomy that she didn't know.

But not this man's, her mind whispered.

"All right," she said finally, pressing her lips together. "I'll untie you." She walked to a closet and took a faded flannel robe from a hook on the door, and laid it across the rocking chair.

"You can put this on. Then I'll come back and help you down the hall to the bathroom."

"I can manage that by myself," he said tersely.

Sarah detected an intense pride in his voice that surprised her and it caused her to reply in a softer, gentler voice than she might have before.

"Don't be foolish about this," she said. "I said I'll come back and help you."

Without looking at him again, she quickly untied his arms and went to the foot of the bed to undo the nylons around his ankles. Her arms brushed against his cold feet and she felt a twinge of guilt.

As soon as he was free she backed away, being careful to keep her scarred face turned away from him. He moved his legs restlessly and rubbed his hands against the bed covers to restore their circulation.

Sarah glanced at him once, then whirled around to leave the room. She wouldn't be surprised if he threw the covers back with nothing on, just to see her reaction. She thought he definitely had a cantankerous streak. And she had the feeling that he was used to doing pretty much as he pleased where women were concerned. She wasn't sure why that thought should surprise her. Or bother her.

In the hallway Sarah waited a few seconds, then tapped on the bedroom door. She heard his muttered reply for her to come in. She didn't know how he had managed to stand on his own but he was standing, although he looked a bit unsteady.

He was taller than she thought and though he was slender, he looked even more powerful standing than he had in bed.

She went across to help him, hesitating only a moment before getting close. She was careful to position herself so that her hair hid the side of her face as she helped support him. He leaned rather heavily on her and she noted how unsteady he was as he walked. He was much weaker than he wanted to admit.

The walk to the bathroom was a short one. The house was small, with only four rooms and a bath. But those few steps left the man breathing heavily and Sarah noticed a thin coating of perspiration on his forehead as she stopped outside the bathroom.

"You sure you can manage alone?" she asked doubtfully.

He gave her a wry look and grunted, then with teeth gritted, he pulled away from her. He stumbled and caught himself with his right arm against the frame of the door. He was so pale that Sarah thought he might pass out right at her feet. But she could see the stubborn determination on his face and she knew he wasn't about to let her go into the bathroom with him, nurse or not.

She couldn't help smiling slightly as she watched him go inside and close the door. She walked down the hallway to the front door and glanced outside. It would be daylight soon. Tom was still sleeping. She could see his long tail curled outside the box. Everything seemed perfectly normal and she was grateful for that.

She waited in the hallway outside the bathroom. What an odd man this stranger was. His look of confusion when he couldn't remember his name had touched her. And yet, in a few moments, he had managed to cover his fears well. Even inject a little sarcastic humor into the conversation.

But was there something in his subconscious...some intuition of who or what he was that made him refuse to let her call the sheriff?

He was in danger. And he didn't trust anyone.

She understood that. Her question was—could *she* trust *him?*

Sarah glanced toward the hall tree. Leaning against it was her grandfather's old shotgun. It wasn't loaded; she would never keep a loaded gun in the house. But now she looked at it thoughtfully. She walked to the hall tree and let her hand rest on the barrel of the gun just as the stranger emerged from the bathroom across from her.

He'd removed the bandage from his head and he looked rather pale, but his eyes when they saw the shotgun, were as flinty and challenging as before.

His gaze moved from the gun up to Sarah's face. He leaned against the door frame, his arms crossed over his chest, although the effort brought a grimace of pain to his face.

"You going to shoot me?"

"I...I...no, of course not. I don't even know how to use a gun."

"Anyone can use a shotgun. Is it loaded?"

Her eyes darted away from the intensity of his gaze and she bit her lower lip before answering him.

"Why...yes."

A slow smile moved over his face. A rather lopsided grin that changed him into a mischievous little boy.

"You're lying," he murmured, his voice soft.

Sarah lifted her chin and looked across the hallway directly into his eyes.

"You couldn't meet my eyes when you said it. And biting your lip was a definite giveaway."

With a small huff of impatience, Sarah straightened and moved away from the shotgun.

"Perhaps you're a psychologist," she said with a hint of sarcasm. "Since you seem to know so much about human nature."

"I wouldn't hurt you," he said. He didn't move, and his expression as he looked at her was more serious.

"How do I know that?" she asked. "How can *you* know it?"

"I know myself. I might not know my name or anything else about my life right now. But I do know one thing—I could never hurt a woman...certainly not one as beautiful as you."

Sarah frowned suddenly and shook her head as if to brush away his words and the ache they brought so inexplicably to her heart.

"Here," she said, her voice gruff. "You need to get back to bed. You're obviously delirious."

She heard his quiet, appreciative grunt of laughter and she smiled, too. She went to him, still careful to shield her scar from him. When she put her arm around him, she felt him flinch as the pain of moving struck him.

"The reason you're so weak is that you lost a lot of blood," she murmured. "Another reason why you should let me call a doctor. I should have brought you a bedpan..." she murmured. But hearing his quiet curses, she stopped, sighing with exasperation at his male pride.

"I know...I know," she said. "You don't need any help."

In the bedroom, she stopped at the rocking chair and motioned for him to sit down.

"Can you sit here a moment while I change the sheets?"

He nodded and she quickly stripped off the blood-stained sheets and replaced them with crisp, clean white ones.

When she got him back into bed, he lay against the pillows and closed his eyes, obviously exhausted. He was still wearing her grandfather's ratty-looking old bathrobe and it gaped open in front, revealing his chest down to his waist.

Sarah couldn't help noticing again how sculpted and toned his muscles were. Or how the dark mat of hair on his chest caught her attention immediately and made her fingers curl unexpectedly into a fist as she wondered at the texture of it.

She made a quiet noise of protest and shook her head. She didn't know what on earth was wrong with her. Maybe Lacy was right—maybe she'd been hidden out here in the country for too long. Away from the real world much too long.

It didn't help that the stranger had opened his eyes and lay watching her with open curiosity and a little quirk of amusement on his lips. For a seriously wounded man who had lost his past, he seemed still to have a rather vigorous sense of humor.

His gaze moved down to his chest, as if he knew exactly what she was thinking. But for once he didn't mock her.

"When I came here," he said, "was there a wallet . . . anything?"

Sarah turned and picked up the clothes she had looked through earlier.

"These are the clothes you were wearing," she said.

He lifted his brows, nodding his approval.

"Nice," he said with that self-deprecating sense of humor.

"There was nothing to identify you. No wallet or ID. Not even a matchbook or change. Someone obviously searched you before . . . before . . ." She stopped, not knowing how he might react to her mention of what had happened to him.

"It's all right," he said. "I don't remember much about that night, so you don't have to tiptoe around the subject."

"The . . . the labels in the shirt and jacket are obviously designer . . . obviously very expensive," she said, holding the clothes toward him.

Hagan frowned and reached up to rub his temples.

"Are you in pain?" she asked.

"No...no," he said. "It's just something..." He shrugged and shook his head. "Somehow I don't feel like a man who can afford expensive designer clothes."

He didn't bother telling her about the flashes he saw in the back of his mind because he didn't understand them himself. The dark littered streets, garbage cans overflowing. The scent of cooking and filthy alley smells that mingled together. There was a kid...a little boy running. Afraid and running. Was it him?

"You've remembered something," she said, her voice hushed.

"No..." he said, waving his hand. "It's nothing...nothing."

Sarah wasn't sure she believed him, but something about the look on his face kept her from pursuing it any further.

"There was one thing," she said.

"What?"

"You said a name...while you were unconscious. Cord...you said 'Find Cord.'" She watched him carefully, trying to read his expression.

"Cord?" He frowned and shook his head. She watched as he tried to remember, gritting his teeth with frustration. His fists against the bed clenched and unclenched.

"Does it mean anything?" she asked.

He shrugged and sighed heavily.

"No."

"It'll come to you," she murmured. "Just relax...give it time."

"I have a feeling I don't have a lot of time," he said.

He looked up at her and his eyes narrowed.

"Why are you standing so far away? Afraid I'll bite?"

"I think this is close enough," Sarah said.

"Would you feel safer if you tied me up again? You'll have to come closer for that." Hagan lifted his arm as an offering to be tied. His eyes glittered with mischief and just a hint of cynicism. He shifted his weight in bed and groaned from the pain in his ribs.

"Oh, I think you're much too weak to be much of a threat to me," she said pointedly. She felt a little safer with him. Still, she didn't intend to let him know that, or to let him see how disconcerted he made her.

"Oh, honey, I wouldn't count on that," he drawled.

Sarah stared into his eyes for a moment. Then she turned to leave the room.

"I'll bring you some juice and cereal and then I'll give you something for your pain. It's best to take it with food."

Hagan lay very quietly after Sarah left the room. What an unusual woman she was. She'd taken him in, with considerable trouble if she were telling the truth about getting him into the house alone. She'd tended his wounds with concern and efficiency. He'd even seen a glint of understanding in her eyes when he asked her not to call the sheriff.

Later, when Sarah returned with a breakfast tray, she placed it on the table beside his bed.

"Sorry it has to be something cold. But since there's no electricity..."

For one unguarded moment as she bent near the bed, she forgot why she had hidden away here at the farm. She forgot to hide the scar she'd received the night her husband died.

Sarah heard him gasp and then curse quietly, and she looked down into his eyes. She had thought they would be hazel or blue, but she could see now that they were black...the deep glittering color of onyx. And there was such a look of horror in their depths that she felt momentarily stunned.

Then she remembered her scar and realized why he was looking at her so strangely.

"Oh," she murmured.

Immediately her hand came up to cover the scar and she backed away from the bed.

"Wait," he said, reaching his hand out toward her.

"I ... I have to go," she said, her voice catching in her throat. "If there's anything else you need, just call. I'll be in the kitchen."

All she wanted was to run. To get away from the look of horror she saw in those black eyes.

Chapter 3

Sarah practically ran out of the house. Despite what she'd told him, she didn't stay in the kitchen where she could hear if he called.

She went outside to the front porch and stood clinging to a post as she tried to catch her breath.

The rain had passed and the morning sun was just breaking through the remaining clouds. Light filtered through the dripping leaves of huge old trees that surrounded the small farmhouse and a light layer of fog wafted in misty streaks across the nearby meadows.

Sarah rubbed her fingers across her eyes. She was tired and confused. And she was stunned at how deeply this stranger's reaction to the scarring on her face had affected her.

She usually wore a scarf or a large hat when she went into town. The man inside was the first totally objective person who'd seen her this way besides her friend Lacy and the people at the hospital.

And he'd been horrified by the ugliness of it.

Well, what did she expect? She could see for herself that she looked like a monstrous freak, with the red puckered scar pulling at the corner of her mouth and giving her face a permanent, one-sided smile.

But it wasn't anything new to her. So why did she suddenly feel like crying? And why had she felt such regret, looking into those intelligent expressive eyes? Such longing. And for what?

"I don't know," she whispered, shaking her head. "I just don't know."

Inside the house, Hagan cursed quietly because he was too weak to go after the woman who had taken him in.

She had completely mistaken his reaction to her scarred face and he felt a wrenching sense of regret. The last thing he ever intended was to put more sadness than there already was in those beautiful eyes.

His cursing had been toward whatever fate had left her scarred and sad. But he realized immediately that she hadn't taken it that way. Didn't she know that even with the scar she was still an incredible-looking woman?

At least now he knew why she was here. Or partly. Hiding away in some lonely old farmhouse. And as he lay there staring at the door, wishing her back, he couldn't help wondering what else she was hiding.

Despite the pain and grief Sarah had suffered the past year, she still a practical woman. When she came back inside the house, she had reconciled herself to the fact that the man had seen the scar. At least now he knew and there was no longer a need to turn her head away from him. Oddly she found that a profound relief.

She walked straight into the bedroom without hesitation and stood at the foot of the bed.

"God, I'm glad you came back," he said, gazing at her with regret in his eyes. "Look, Sarah..."

"It's all right," she said, her voice cool. "You don't have to say anything. I know how awful it looks."

"I was surprised, that's all."

"Sure," she said.

"Sarah, I think it looks worse to you than it does to anyone else."

She noticed that the electric lamp was burning beside the bed. Wanting to change the subject, she said, "At least the electricity has come back on. If you'd rather have something hot to eat I can—"

"Sit down," he said, nodding toward the chair.

"Really, I have things to do. I—"

"What things?" he asked impatiently. "Don't tell me you're going to plow the north forty this morning. Not that I'd be surprised. You're quite a little bundle of energy, aren't you?" His eyes moved slowly over. "Or is that busy stuff just to avoid me?"

With an impatient shrug she sat in the rocker, leaning forward as if she might dart from the room at any moment. But she didn't bother trying to hide her face from him.

"What happened?" he asked, his eyes moving to the scar.

"A car accident."

"Recently?"

She sighed heavily. This was not a conversation she really wanted to have.

"A year ago," she said.

"You're a beautiful woman," he said quietly. "I'm surprised the doctors haven't suggested plastic surgery."

"They have," she said in a dry, monotone voice.

"Then why—?"

"Maybe because I don't much give a damn how I look anymore...all right?" She stood up suddenly. Her lips were clamped together as she stared defensively at him.

Somehow she hadn't expected him to be so openly inquisitive about her scar. Most people would just pretend it wasn't there.

Hagan's eyes narrowed as he studied her expression and the way her hands clenched into tight little fists at her sides.

"And why is it that you don't...give a damn?" he asked, his voice soft and patient.

"That's really none of your business."

"You're right...it isn't," he said.

Sarah noted a difference in the tone of his voice. The earlier cockiness and teasing were gone and she felt a little twinge of guilt for being so hateful.

"I'm sorry," he said.

"There's no reason to be sorry," she said. "I'm doing just fine. Now, let's talk about something else, shall we? You, for instance, and what I'm going to do about you."

Hagan was surprised by her attitude. What an unusual woman she was. He had seen the sadness in her eyes earlier when she ran from the room, so her declaration that she didn't give a damn just didn't ring true. She obviously did care. Yet now she was acting as if nothing had happened. As if the terrible scar meant nothing to her.

She'd shielded her face from him all last night, but now that he'd seen it, she stood proudly before him. Openly defiant, even. As if she dared him to say anything.

He bit his lip as he studied her beautiful, haughty face.

"What?" she asked sharply.

"Nothing," he said with a shake of his head. "This is obviously a subject you don't want to discuss, so we won't...until you're ready. You were trying to decide what to do about me?"

Sarah opened her mouth to say something. She was frowning at him. He could be so damn unpredictable.

"I wanted to ask you about a doctor, one last time. I know several personally at the hospital who would be willing to come out here. You could trust any one of them—"

"No," he said, shaking his head. "I'm sure you can trust these doctors, but right now I can't afford to take such a chance."

"But you can't tell me why you feel this way. You don't even know why yourself."

"That's right—I don't."

He watched Sarah's expression, saw the struggle going on inside her. And somehow instinctively he knew he'd always been able to convince women when he needed to. So, why didn't that reassure him about this woman?

"Look," he said. "I just need a little time. Maybe this is only temporary...maybe I'll just wake up in the morning and everything will have come back to me."

"That's possible," she mused. "Although I don't think—"

"Will you give me a little time?" he asked. "A few hours...a day? I can't give you a good solid reason for doing that. But some gut instinct tells me that I shouldn't contact the sheriff. And to be honest, that might be because I'm the biggest crook in the nation."

Sarah frowned at him. She had her own reasons not to trust the sheriff. She resented the fact that he had never followed up on the accident or tried to find the truck that sideswiped them. He'd never even really seemed to take her story seriously, insisting it was a drunk driver who hit them.

He had brushed aside her belief that the truck had rammed them deliberately. And her fear that it had something to do with the undercover story Joe was working on had simply been ignored.

But nothing the sheriff said would ever convince her that she was wrong. And perhaps if she had lost her memory she'd still retain that strong feeling of distrust. The same way this man felt a deep-seated, intuitive distrust.

"I'd know," he said, watching her and seeing her inner turmoil. "If I had done something wrong or dishonest, memory or not, I'd know it, wouldn't I?"

Sarah nodded. "Maybe. A person's character doesn't change just because he has amnesia."

If she believed in anything anymore, it was that instincts were real and viable. And she knew that the earnestness she saw in his eyes could not be faked. Other than that, she couldn't explain why she was inclined to agree to his request for more time.

"All right," she said finally. "On one condition."

"And that is?"

"That you rest and take the medicine I give you. And that you tell me immediately if you have any unusual symptoms such as excruciating headaches or shortness of breath."

"I'm not even going to ask what those symptoms would indicate," he said dryly. "But I agree."

"Good. In the meantime, I'll listen to the news and perhaps later I can drive into town and get a newspaper. Someone is bound to be missing you by now. Do you have any feelings about that? Any instincts about a family... a wife?" she added quietly.

Hagan hadn't thought about the possibility that he could have a wife or a family.

His gaze moved over her face, coming to rest on her full lips.

"My instincts tell me very clearly..." his black eyes moved up to meet her startled gaze "...that I love women. But as to a wife...no...I think probably I'm a loner."

"You could be wrong."

"I'm never wrong." His eyes, steady and intense, stared straight into hers.

She was caught for long, heart-stopping moments by those eyes. And by the deep resonance of his voice.

"I should bring you some pain medication."

She turned and hurried from the room. In the kitchen it took long moments before she managed to compose herself enough to return to his room.

She handed him a glass of water and some tablets.

"What is it?" he asked.

"Just painkiller. Nothing exotic...hospital-strength Tylenol. It'll help you rest."

Hagan shook his head, taking the water, but ignoring the pills in Sarah's hand.

"I don't need it. Something could happen. I might need to be alert and those would only dull my mind and my reflexes."

Sarah sighed with exasperation. What kind of life did he have that he was so cautious...so concerned with being on guard every moment?

"Have you already forgotten our agreement?" she reminded him. "This will relax you and take the pain away. You probably have a concussion and I know your head must ache terribly. And whether you know it or not, you are aware of that pain even in your sleep, which means you won't rest properly." Her voice grew softer and more cajoling. "Nothing's going to happen. You're safe here. So please...take it."

She almost laughed when he grimaced, then reached out to take the medicine. Still, she watched him carefully as he drank the water and swallowed the tablets. When she took the glass of water from him, she gently opened his fingers to make sure he hadn't hidden the pills.

"Why Miss Sarah," he drawled, his eyes wide. "Don't tell me you still don't trust me."

"Should I?" she replied.

Hagan chuckled and slid down into the bed. Then he reached toward her.

The movement surprised her and she hesitated for a moment, staring at his outstretched hand.

Finally, against her better judgment, she took his hand. His fingers were warm and strong and there was something compelling about his look and his touch.

"Sarah James," he said, his voice soft.

"What?"

"Thank you," he said, pulling her closer. "For saving my life. And for letting me stay. For trusting me enough to untie me. There's nothing I hate worse than being tied down," he added with a teasing smile.

"Ah . . . see," she said. "Something else you remember about yourself. Do you think you meant that figuratively, or literally?" she added.

"Both, I think," he said with a grin.

Sarah nodded. She probably shouldn't trust him. Every nerve in her body was warning her not to.

In fact she was beginning to think that this man, whoever he was, was the last man on earth she should trust.

When he closed his eyes, Sarah went into the kitchen to make herself a cup of tea. She sat at her grandmother's old kitchen table and traced patterns on the red checked oilcloth the way she'd done when she was a girl.

Her thoughts were about the man lying in her front bedroom. About the way he had been tied when she found him. Who was he and why had someone wanted him dead?

He seemed confident that he would wake up and remember everything and she hoped for his sake that it happened. But she hadn't the heart to tell him how unlikely it was. It would take time. And it might not ever happen at all.

Sarah got up and walked to the counter to turn on a small radio. As she listened to the music and sipped her tea, her mind wandered. But when the announcement of the news came, she listened carefully.

The man's voice droned monotonously as he acknowledged the advertising sponsors, but Sarah noticed there was a decided note of interest in his tone when he began to tell what he described as the story of the hour. Nothing important ever happened in Wayland. And he made this sound important.

"At dawn this morning, agents with the Georgia Bureau of Investigation raided a backwoods compound on the Satilla River. It has long been rumored that a cultlike group living there was involved in illegal activities from drugs to gun smuggling. The raid came after an apparent botched undercover operation last night during which a young female policewoman, Cynthia Harper, from Atlanta, was killed. Witnesses say she was pushed from a speeding van on Highway 82 just outside Wayland. Police have not confirmed the story and are releasing no other information, although sources tell us another undercover G.B.I. agent was believed still inside the van when it eluded law-enforcement officers. The Georgia Bureau of Investigation will not confirm or deny it, although there was a very intense search in the area last night, which was called off because of heavy rain that has flooded area streams. Officers are also on a manhunt for the occupants of the dark green van described by witnesses. Ware County

Sheriff, Ben Metcalf, will have a statement about the case today at noon."

Sarah sank back in her chair. She'd been holding her breath and now, as the reality of what the announcer said sunk in, she felt stunned.

Could the man in her house be the missing agent? Or was he perhaps one of the others...someone from the van?

She glanced at her watch. It was ten o'clock. She'd make sure he was awake at noon so he could hear the report for himself. Maybe something about it would trigger a memory for him.

"My gosh," she murmured. "This is unbelievable."

She glanced through the wide arched door of the kitchen and down the hallway, toward the room where the stranger lay. When the phone in the kitchen rang, Sarah almost jumped out of her skin and she picked it up quickly.

"Sarah?"

"Oh...Lacy," Sarah said breathlessly.

"I've been worried to death about you."

"Why?" Sarah said, suddenly alert and cautious.

"You didn't call me last night when you got home. You said you would...don't you remember? The storm was terrible. I felt guilty that I'd coerced you into coming for dinner and you had to drive home in that."

"The phone was out," Sarah said. At least that was the truth. "Actually I didn't even know it was working again until just now." She glanced down the hall, hoping the phone hadn't wakened her patient. He needed rest more than anything.

"I was just getting ready to drive out there and make sure you were all right."

"Oh, heavens," Sarah said, her voice breathless with anxiety. "I'm glad you didn't do that. There's no need...I'm fine. What shift are you on today?" she asked, intending to change the subject.

Sarah and Lacy had grown up together. They'd gone through nursing school together and ended up working at the same hospital.

"Second." There was an odd tone to Lacy's voice. "I told you that last night."

"Oh, yes, that's right, you did."

"Sarah...is everything all right?"

"Of course...everything's fine."

Get it together Sarah, she warned herself. Lacy knows you better than anyone and if anyone is going to pick up on your mood and become suspicious, it will be her.

"Really," Sarah said. "I'm just tired. I didn't get much sleep last night...because of the storm." She frowned, hoping Lacy would believe her.

"I know. Me, too. Comes from working at the hospital, I guess. Seems like all the bad things happen on rainy nights. Early babies, domestic quarrels and car accidents. Did you hear about the woman they found outside town?" She skimmed right past Sarah's murmur that she had. "It's just horrible. Really scary. I spoke to Ruth in E.R. and she said the girl was young and very pretty. Everyone's in an uproar over it because the news about her leaked out. Law enforcement's blaming the hospital and the hospital's gone into it's defense mode. There's even a rumor that the G.B.I. is investigating Sheriff Metcalf's office because of a leak that messed up the undercover operation."

"You're kidding."

"That's what I hear. Well, look, I have a million things to do. Mother wants me to take her to the bank. Are you sure you're all right? I can still drive out later. I could bring lunch if you'd like and—"

"No...no," Sarah said. "You don't have to do that. Besides, I think I'll go back to bed for a while."

"Hey," Lacy said, her voice slower and softer. "I'm really glad you came to dinner last night. This is what it's going to take, you know. A dinner here and there, a movie or two, and soon you'll be ready to think about having your surgery and coming back to work."

"I hope so," Sarah said.

"Call me," Lacy said as she hung up.

Sarah walked out to the front porch. She closed her eyes and breathed in the sweet scent of wild roses and the rain that still clung to the trees and shrubbery around the old house. She fed the cat and walked to the edge of the porch to make sure nothing of her truck could be seen through the closed garage doors that hung rather haphazardly on their old hinges.

She should try to sleep, she knew that. But glancing out toward the road and beyond where she'd seen the van, she thought that would be impossible.

She glanced at her watch and went to the kitchen to make soup for her patient. It would be time for the newscast before she knew it and she wanted to make sure he ate before he heard everything.

If he really was this missing agent, he was not going to like the news one bit. And if he was in that van, he probably saw the female officer murdered. That in itself could explain his amnesia. It could be that he didn't *want* to remember.

Later she tiptoed into his room with the tray of food, then hurried back to the kitchen to bring the old radio. After plugging it into the outlet, she walked to the bed and turned on a light. Her patient's eyes were closed and he seemed to be breathing quietly.

"You don't have to tiptoe," he said. The sudden sound of his deep voice in the quiet room caused her to jump. His lashes lifted and she found herself staring into those incredible eyes.

"I brought you some soup... and a radio. There's going to be a news conference in a few minutes about something that happened last night. I thought you should hear it."

Hagan frowned and tired to push himself up in bed. He groaned slightly and winced.

"Be careful," Sarah began, her hand reaching toward him. "Don't..."

"I'm all right," he snapped. "You don't have to baby me. I'm not used to it."

Sarah's lips tightened and she felt a flush cover her face.

"You don't have to feed me, either. Just stop hovering," he said.

She handed him a glass of ice tea and watched as he placed it against his forehead and closed his eyes. Ignoring any further protests, she placed the back of her hand against his face.

He felt hot... too hot.

"Wait...don't drink that yet," she said. "I need to take your temperature first."

"Forget it," he said. "I'm fine."

Sarah couldn't decide what made him so grumpy, except that what he said about being babied was probably true. With his male ego that was probably enough to make him irritable. Not to mention the fact that he was wounded and had a fever. No matter how detached he seemed to be, she knew he had to be feeling anxious about who he was. Sometimes with an amnesiac victim, their subconscious voice spoke volumes about who they were. She'd just have to be sure she listened carefully for any hints of what that inner voice might be telling him.

Sarah took the glass of tea from his hand just as he started to drink it.

"Look, if you don't want to go the hospital, then I'm afraid you're stuck with me," she said. "And that means you're going to have to stick to our agreement and do exactly as I say if you want to get better." She almost smiled at his look of disbelief. He obviously was not used to being told what to do, either.

"Well? You do want to get better, don't you?"

Her patient rolled his eyes and gave a loud huff of indignation, then he shrugged.

"You're enjoying this," he muttered.

"Yes, as a matter of fact, I am," she said.

"All right... all right," he grumbled. "Take the damn temperature."

Sarah frowned when she read the numbers.

"A hundred and two," she said quietly. "That's not good." She placed the tray cross his lap. "Can you manage?" she asked automatically.

She was very close to him and as she glanced at his face, she was looking directly into his eyes. The frustration and spark of defiance was still burning as brightly as ever.

"What a silly question," she murmured as she straightened and stared at him. "Of course you can manage. You're a big tough guy, aren't you? And you don't need anyone's help."

Hagan's eyebrow lifted slightly, but he ignored her as he began awkwardly spooning soup into his mouth. Sarah noticed that he hardly moved his head and she thought it must be hurting him badly. Not that he would ever admit it.

Sarah rummaged in her nurse's bag and brought two tablets to him.

"More Tylenol," she said. "It will help keep your fever down. But I have to tell you that you probably have an infection, which is very common with gunshot wounds—especially if you happened to lay in or swallow the swamp water last night." Sarah grimaced at the thought. "I can get some antibiotics but they might not be strong enough to get rid of it. You really should be getting them in an IV drip, especially since you lost so much blood," she said almost to herself.

"Go ahead," he said. "Hook me up."

"It's not quite that easy," she murmured. "I don't just happen to have such material lying around here at the farm."

"Then this will have to do," he said.

Sarah shook her head helplessly. She could use different herbal teas from the garden to strengthen his immune system and her grandmother's liniment made from lobelia would be good for his bruises. Other than that there wasn't much else she could do.

He took the tablets, then glanced at a clock beside the bed. Impatiently he pushed the tray away from him.

"You said there's a news conference?"

Sarah turned on the radio and sat in the rocking chair, well away from the bed. She felt like a voyeur as she watched him listening to the same news text she'd heard that morning. He frowned a time or two, but she could read nothing in his expression. When the announcer got to the part about the woman officer who'd been killed, Sarah saw him tense. He stared hard at the radio and this time he wasn't able to disguise the pain in his eyes. His jaw tightened and released and when he turned to meet her gaze, she thought she'd never seen such fury, or such agony.

"Did it mean anything to you?" she asked.

He pushed his hand over his unshaven jaw and chin, closing his eyes with a sigh of exasperation.

"I don't know. No," he said.

"They said they think the other agent is missing," she said, still watching his expression.

"And you think that might be me," he said with a soft grunt of doubt.

"I don't know. Maybe. Last night when I was driving home I saw a dark green van coming toward me. It seemed to be stopped on the side of the road about a mile from the house here."

"That's stretching it a bit," he said. "I'm sure there are a lot of green vans around."

"I know...but you have to come from somewhere. There's no car. Maybe you got away from them somehow. Maybe they shot at you as you ran through the brush and swamp water."

Hagan frowned as he recalled the vision he'd had earlier. The rain and wet brush slapping against him as he stumbled and fell, then pushed himself up and tried to run again.

"And I heard something, too," she continued. "Just before the van revved up and sped past me toward town. It could have been a gunshot."

Hagan shook his head and his eyes turned brooding and thoughtful.

"What?" she asked. "What are you thinking?"

"I know guns," he said. His eyes stared straight ahead, blank and expressionless. "When I saw your shotgun in the hallway earlier, I realized that I know an awful lot about guns. Ruegers, Smith & Wessons...gun clips and single shot. Automatics and semis..." His voice trailed away in a puzzled monotone.

"A G.B.I. agent would certainly know about guns," she offered softly.

He turned to look at her, his eyes searching and troubled.

"So would a gunrunner. And he'd be much more likely to be wearing those clothes you showed me earlier."

Chapter 4

Sarah couldn't deny that what he was saying was true. But she still didn't want to believe he was a criminal.

Hagan's expression softened slightly as he looked at Sarah and at the mysterious scar that troubled her so. Here was a woman who had her own problems. Yet she had taken him in, without thought for her own safety. She had treated him as tenderly as anyone could. Whatever he was involved in, now she was involved in it, too. That was the part that bothered him.

Even now as he made the suggestion that he could be a criminal, she was looking at him with sympathy and understanding.

"Look," he said, swallowing hard. "I'm sorry if I seem ungrateful for all you've done. I'm not, believe me. It's just that I'm so damn frustrated. Whoever I am, I don't think I'm used to being on the sidelines, waiting for someone to rescue me or take care of me."

"I'd say you're right about that."

Just then the announcement that the sheriff's statement was imminent made both of them stop and glance toward the radio.

"I wonder what he'll say?" Sarah said. "A friend of mine called this morning and she said—"

"A friend?" Hagan snapped, tensing. "Called you? What did you tell her?"

"Don't worry," Sarah said, her voice turning wry and a bit sarcastic. "I didn't tell her that I found a mysterious man on my porch after I got home last night. Or that I dragged him into the house where he's lying in my grandparent's bed complaining because he's been shot and can't be up and about. Who'd ever believe such a wild story?"

Hagan closed his eyes and shook his head. There was a little hint of a smile on his lips when he looked at her again.

"Sorry. Second nature maybe...being cautious. Go ahead...tell me what your friend said about the sheriff."

"She said there were rumors that the G.B.I. is investigating Sheriff Metcalf's office. That he might somehow be involved in the leak that caused the undercover operation to go wrong last night."

"That's probably a mistake," he murmured. He seemed lost in thought as he rubbed his hand over his jaw.

"What? You think it's a mistake to suspect the sheriff?"

"I think it's a mistake to let him know they're investigating him. That's undoubtedly what his announcement is going to be about. He's defending himself. Without meaning to, the agency has given him a chance to make the first move. I don't think that's the way I'd have handled it."

Sarah lifted her eyebrows and grinned at him.

"See...you seem to know an awful lot about law enforcement procedures."

He only grimaced and shook his head doubtfully.

Sarah recognized the sheriff's voice as he began to speak.

"I have a statement about the undercover operation in our county, which resulted in the tragic death of a young police officer named Cynthia Harper. I would like to put a stop to any rumors circulating about whether or not the Ware County Sheriff's Department is fully involved in this investigation. We are cooperating completely with the G.B.I. and the F.B.I., as we always do in such circumstances. We will continue to work with them to find Ms. Harper's murderers."

Sarah winced at the words and turned to look at her mystery man. He was transfixed, sitting tensely, completely unmoving as he listened.

The sheriff's voice went on.

"Deputies from Ware County assisted last night in the raid on the Satilla River Compound and will continue to assist wherever we are needed. That's all I have to say, folks. Thank you."

"Sheriff... Sheriff!" the reporters shouted. "What about the other G.B.I. agent who's reported missing? Can you give us any information about him? His name or where he's from?"

"Until the case is solved, our office will have no further statements."

"Well," Sarah said, her eyes wide with curiosity. "What do you think about that? Did any of what he said mean anything?"

"No, I can't say it did, although..."

"What?"

"Nothing." The flashes of light behind his eyes... the memories of running through the rain didn't mean anything concrete to him. Not yet, anyway.

Sarah couldn't help feeling disappointed.

"You said earlier that you saw a van," he said.

"Yes, I did," she said.

"I'm not saying this van was the one the law is looking for," he said. "Or that it had anything to do with what happened to me. If I was ever in a van I don't remember it. But let's suppose it was the one. Let's suppose you're right and that you scared them off and gave me a chance to run. If you saw them, then they saw you, too. They know the kind of vehicle you drive. If they come back looking for a body it could be only a matter of time before they see your car and put two and two together. They could come knocking at your door and this time they'll make sure they finish the job."

Sarah listened speechlessly. His words brought a feeling of impending doom. She hadn't expected this. Somehow, without even knowing who this man was, she had felt safer with him here. And now, hearing that might not be the case, she felt more scared than she had since the whole thing began.

"I hid the truck," she said, her mind whirling as she tried to think.

His gaze turned on her as if for a moment he didn't understand.

"You what?"

"I was driving a truck. I hid it . . . for the same reasons you just mentioned. Last night . . . it was still dark and I . . . I locked it in the garage. I don't know why exactly. I just didn't think it was a good idea to leave it out in plain view."

"Good," Hagan said. "Good thinking." He breathed an audible sigh of relief. "It'll buy a little time at least. But look, I can't let you become any more involved in this than you already are. It's too dangerous. I have to get out of here before someone comes looking for me.''

"You can't possibly leave," she protested. "You have a fever and you've lost too much blood. You wouldn't be able to walk a hundred yards."

Hagan sighed heavily, but he didn't argue.

"Besides, where would you go? You have no name. You can't remember where you live. I could give you money, but it wouldn't last long. It looks as if you have only two choices. Call the sheriff's office . . . or stay here."

"Listen to me," he said. "You have no idea how dangerous this could be for you. If someone wants me dead, they're not going to stop until they've accomplished that. And I don't want you in the way when that happens."

Sarah's eyes widened, sparkling now with some hidden fire.

"If," she said fiercely. *"If* that happens. Besides, I'm not going to let someone just walk in here and kill you," she declared. "And whatever I have to do to keep that from happening, that's what I'm going to do. Between the two of us, surely we can figure out who you are before anything else happens."

Hagan saw the determination in her eyes and he knew she meant what she said. Her small body was tensed and ready for action. But he was afraid she had no idea what she was getting herself into.

What he saw in her eyes now made him curious. She had said she didn't care about anything anymore. But right now he would swear that she did care. That her eyes were filled with concern and compassion and a burning determination.

He wasn't sure anyone had ever been willing to give him so much before.

He leaned his head back and closed his eyes. The constant pain in his head was making him weary and he found that despite the dilemma he faced, he hadn't the strength to fight sleep any longer.

"I don't like it," he muttered. "But I'm afraid you're right . . . I'm just too damn tired right now to argue."

"Good," she said.

He watched through narrowed, sleep-filled eyes, as she touched the scar on her face. He had noticed that she did that a lot when she was thoughtful or distracted.

"Sarah . . . come here," he said.

She looked surprised at his softly spoken command. But slowly she moved from the rocking chair so she could stand beside his bed.

Hagan took her hand and pulled her down until she was sitting beside him.

"I have no right to ask you to trust me," he said. "Blind trust is really what I'm asking. But I swear, I would never hurt you, or intentionally involve you in anything that might put you in danger."

Sarah nodded, but the sudden lump in her throat kept her from answering.

"If something happens . . . if someone comes for me, you have to do exactly as I say."

A look of alarm leapt into her beautiful blue eyes and for a moment he thought about changing his mind. He should just leave here and take his chances. No matter what she thought or how much she protested.

"Sarah . . ." he said gently.

He thought it must be the effects of the fever that made him feel the way he did. He let his gaze move over Sarah's auburn hair and over her face. He had hardly been able to miss her slight, deliciously formed figure, from small perfect breasts to slightly curved hips. For a small woman, her legs, encased in snug jeans, looked long and shapely.

When his gaze moved back up to her face, he saw that sad, almost self-defeated look in her eyes. It was one he'd seen before and he found himself wanting to change it more than he'd ever wanted anything.

"You just say the word," he said, "and I'll find some other way out of this mess."

"No," she said quickly and firmly. "I can help you...I know I can. And I want to help you. Besides, you don't have much choice about it, considering your amnesia and the condition you're in. So just stop worrying about me and concentrate on getting better."

His gaze was so intense...so personal that she had to pull her eyes away. But he continued to study her. Her gaze darted toward him, then away as she got up and began to smooth the covers on the bed.

"Didn't anyone ever tell you it's not polite to stare?" she said finally, her voice soft and quiet.

She was close. So close that Hagan caught the scent of her hair. The same scent of wild roses he'd smelled before. He didn't know if it was that or her sweetness, her willingness to help a total stranger, that touched him. But he was surprised to feel his body responding so quickly and so hotly after all he'd been through.

"You are one beautiful woman," he said. "You must know that by now. It would be hard for any man not to stare."

She shook her head and gave him a look of disapproval as if she didn't believe him. Again, as if it were an automatic response, her hand moved up to her cheek.

"Don't," he said. He reached out and put his hand around her wrist. "Don't do that. You don't have to hide anything from me."

Hagan's husky voice sent shivers down Sarah's spine. She looked down to where his fingers held her wrist. His hand was dark in contrast to her paler skin, and surprisingly strong. She couldn't fight the wild tingles of alarm that raced through her body.

His eyes were bright and there was a flush on his dark skin.

It was the fever, she told herself. That was the only reason he was looking at her with such intensity.

Hagan pulled her down beside him again and Sarah, looking into those expressive, mysterious eyes, found she couldn't resist. So many things had happened in the last twenty-four hours. Was it the danger that caused these confusing feelings to wash over her?

For the briefest of moments she wondered how it would feel to touch him the way a woman touches a man. To lie next to him and feel herself encased in those strong, muscular arms. To touch his face . . . and mouth.

"Stay here with me," he whispered.

Sarah could feel his hand shaking from the fever. And as his eyes closed, then opened again, she warned herself against attributing his actions to anything else. He was very ill and close to exhaustion.

Somehow she knew it wasn't his nature to give in to neediness, or to ask anyone for anything. Tomorrow, he might not even remember asking her to stay.

"Just for a while," he whispered, his voice growing rough with weariness. "Until I'm asleep."

Sarah blinked her eyes. Somehow this vulnerability touched her as nothing else could. He was so changeable. So unpredictable that she hardly knew what to expect from him from one moment until the next.

She had not expected the danger in his eyes to retreat so quickly, or for it to be replaced by something even more compelling.

That little-boy quality moved her. And the need she saw in his eyes. It was the one thing about a man she couldn't resist.

She tried to warn herself that he was probably a very clever man. Used to charming people to get his way, she thought. Was that all this was now? Was he such a master at reading people that he'd seen from the beginning what it took to get her cooperation?

Somehow Sarah's mind wouldn't let her answer that question, or examine it too closely. She sat on the bed beside him, looking into eyes that were growing glazed and sleepy. She didn't pull away from his grasp, but sat quietly, feeling the heat from his fevered body through the sheets where her hip touched his.

"It's all right," she whispered as he closed his eyes. "I'm here. I won't leave."

She watched the way a slight smile tugged at the corner of his sensuous mouth, the way his lashes moved, then were still. But even after he was asleep, she didn't pull away.

Without thinking, she reached out to brush the dark hair away from his forehead. Now that it was dry, she could see golden sunstreaks in it. His hair felt soft and rich against her fingers as she traced those pale glints.

With a bemused look, she let her fingers move lower, not touching his long thick lashes, but hovering just above them. She moved her hand toward his mouth and felt the whisper of his breath against her fingers.

She shivered as unexpected visions and fantasies shot quickly through her mind.

How would it feel to bend and kiss those lips? To have him open his mouth beneath hers? Open his beautiful eyes and gaze at her with surprise and pleasure?

The thought made her close her eyes and take a long shuddering breath. In her mind she could see it all so clearly. A vision of them together. Kissing, touching, moving on this very bed in a quick, heated dance of passion.

It was a forbidden fantasy. Impossible. But one moment in a lifetime to daydream about and remember when he was gone. One exciting, forbidden memory to cherish when she was old and alone.

The thoughts were making it difficult for her to breath.

She opened her eyes quickly and moved her hand away from him. Suddenly, as the realization of what she wanted struck her, she stood up, stumbling back in the room until the back of her knees hit the rocking chair and sent it into a ghostly motion.

"My God," she whispered, horrified at her own mind's treacherous thoughts and visions.

She had never felt this way in her life. Never experienced such a delicious, hot feeling of spiraling completely out of control. She had come close with Joe, but somehow had never made it over that sweet, mysterious precipice.

Her wonderful, precious Joe, whom she had loved since childhood.

Thinking of him shook her and brought a terrible bleak cloud of guilt crashing down over her. How could she even compare this stranger...this tough-talking loner to her sweet, gentle husband?

She had to keep her distance from this man. And not just because he was a stranger without a past.

How could she possibly think she knew him or knew what he was? Just because she wanted him to be this missing agent didn't mean that he was. Just because she looked into those eyes and thought she could trust him didn't mean it was true.

It was obviously her mind's way of trying to fool her, to make her think it was all right to flirt with such fantasies. Simply because he was handsome and charming... and sexually appealing.

All of that bothered her, it was true. But not nearly as much as the idea of betraying Joe's memory so quickly and so easily with the first man who came into her life.

This man was a rebel. Even without knowing him she sensed that much. He was an extremely masculine man who liked adventures and knew a lot about guns and women.

It would be so easy to fall into his arms and into his bed. He would welcome her; she'd seen that much in his eyes.

But for how long? Until tomorrow? Until someone came to arrest him ... or kill him? Until she woke up one morning and he was gone with no goodbye and no explanation?

She had thought she could never be with another man after Joe died. But now, with the disturbing realization that she was wrong confronting her, she had to step back. Had to think about what she was doing and where her life was going from here.

She would have to regard this man as untouchable. As a stranger who came into her life one rainy Georgia night only because he needed her help. Under other circumstances, he probably wouldn't look at her twice.

He was a stranger. A handsome forbidden man and one far too dangerous for any woman's peace of mind.

Chapter 5

The stranger slept most of the afternoon and Sarah was glad. It would give her time to think and to put everything into perspective.

She was troubled about her surprisingly intense response to him. She didn't know what had made her have such erotic thoughts about someone she hardly knew.

She was very tired from lack of sleep, but she went outside to work in the garden anyway. She needed the sunshine and fresh air to give her a sense of reality again. She needed the feeling of accomplishment that seeing the neat rows of sprouting seeds brought and the tranquillity that digging in the rich black dirt always gave her.

Tom followed her to the small patch of garden, rubbing against her legs. When she paid him little attention, he plopped down in the damp soil and rolled around playfully before lying still, sleepily watching her work.

The ground was much too wet to work with, but Sarah pulled weeds. The rain had made that task easier, anyway.

As she worked, she tossed small clumps of dirt at the cat and laughed when he batted the pieces back and forth.

"Hey, you silly cat," she said. "What do you think about this dilemma I find myself in?"

Tom meowed and rolled over, his eyes half closed against the bright sun. Sarah reached out and stroked his warm fur.

"My patient is certainly a mystery," she said softly. "And I don't think he trusts anyone very much. Kind of like you when you came here... remember? He could be lying. He could have been involved in what happened last night and knowing that this agent is missing, he could simply be faking his amnesia so I won't turn him in."

Sarah glanced at the house and a shiver ran down her spine.

"I don't really think that's the case, but..."

She didn't want to believe it was anyway. She knew in her heart that she wanted to believe this man was good and decent. She wanted to believe everything her instincts told her about him. But in her head... that was a different matter.

Was she being foolish? Too trusting and idealistic?

"I don't know, Tom," she whispered. "I just don't know."

Tom meowed again and Sarah smiled, then went back to pulling weeds from around the neatly spaced patches of herbs. A few moments later, when she heard the sound of a car, she stopped and glanced toward the highway. What happened last night had made her apprehensive and acutely aware of every car that passed on the seldom used road in front of the house.

This particular car sounded as if it were slowing and when the brown-and-gold car with the star on the door came into sight, Sarah gasped softly and looked toward the house.

Normally seeing the sheriff's car wouldn't make her feel so nervous, but today her insides were trembling.

When the car stopped in her driveway, Sarah stood up and with the back of her glove, brushed her hair out of her eyes.

"Don't look at the house, Sarah," she cautioned herself as she began to walk forward. "Just relax...be cool."

It was Sheriff Metcalf himself who stepped out of the patrol car. He was alone.

"Afternoon, Sarah," he said. He looked around, his eyes seeming to scan every inch of the place as he walked toward her.

"Good afternoon," she said, hoping her voice didn't sound as shaky as she felt. She touched the scar, then shook her head slightly.

Sheriff Metcalf had seen her several times since the accident, so the scar wasn't anything new to him. He'd come to the hospital after the accident and also to offer his condolences about Joe. That's when he'd told her they had no clues about the "drunk driver" who ran them off the road.

As the sheriff approached the small plot of garden where Sarah stood, Tom jumped up and with his bushy tail held high, ran through the grass toward the garage.

"Well," the sheriff drawled. "Got a cat now, I see. He doesn't seem to take to strangers much." He laughed and his face crinkled good-naturedly.

"No, I guess not," Sarah said. "He's just not very sociable, I guess," she said. She took off her gardening gloves and wiped her hands nervously down her pant legs. It took every ounce of strength she possessed to keep from glancing toward the house and the windows of the room where her mysterious patient slept.

Sarah turned her attention toward the sheriff. He was still smiling.

Like most people who grew up in Ware County, she had known Sheriff Metcalf all her life. But she was probably one of the few people who didn't trust him. Until the accident she'd thought he was a good, dedicated lawman, one to be admired and respected. But his attitude after Joe's death changed all that for her.

Having him here in front of her, his tall form straight and dignified, his eyes gazing kindly at her, Sarah wavered a bit about her feelings. It would be hard for anyone to suspect this man of doing anything wrong. And she couldn't quite explain why she did, except for some deep gut feeling.

"How you been, Sarah?" the sheriff asked.

"Me? Oh . . . I'm doing fine," she said, forcing herself to smile. "Just fine."

"I was driving by and thought I'd stop in and check on you," he said.

"Well, I appreciate that."

"Everyone in town expected you'd be back at work by now."

"Yes . . . I know." Sarah glanced down at the gloves she held in her hands. It might be nice living in a small town, but one of the disadvantages was that everyone knew your business. And no one seemed to mind offering advice about what they thought was best for you.

The sheriff sighed and put his hands on his hips. The service revolver he wore strapped at his side looked large and ominous.

"Just don't seem right out here without your granddad," he said, looking around at the farm. "But everyone said he wouldn't last long after your grandma Grace died."

"They were crazy about each other," Sarah agreed, smiling wistfully. "Even after having been married more than fifty years."

"Yep. Guess you can't say that about many folks these days."

Sarah began to feel uneasy. The sheriff seemed to be stalling and his alert eyes were scanning every inch of the property, as if to see if something were out of place. He looked toward the house, his eyes narrowed and in shadows beneath a white wide-brimmed cowboy hat.

She hadn't closed the door to the front bedroom.

Dear God, what if the sheriff asked to come inside?

He turned his gaze back to her.

"Listen," he said. "We had something happen here in the county last night. I don't mean to alarm you, but it might not be a good idea for you to stay out here, all by yourself. You still got your old place in town, don't you?"

"Yes, I do," Sarah said. "It's rented to a young couple."

"Too bad. Thought you might want to stay there awhile. You didn't hear anything unusual last night, did you? See anyone hangin' around? Passin' by on the road maybe?"

The suspicious tone in his voice caused Sarah's heart to skip a beat.

"No," she said. "I haven't seen anyone."

He smiled again and Sarah reached up to touch her throat. She wondered how much he'd tell her.

"Does this have anything to do with the raid on the Satilla River?" she asked. "I heard about it on the news this morning."

"Did you?" he asked casually. "Yeah...'s bad business, that bunch out there. But I don't think you have to worry about them so much as the two who escaped. The ones who were in the van."

"Do...do you think they might be in this area?" Sarah asked, her voice breathless.

"Could be." He seemed cautious and very serious. "Could be anywhere. They killed a woman police officer from Atlanta. Guess you heard about that, too?"

"Yes...I did. It's just terrible." Sarah forced herself to meet his eyes. "Who'd think that something like that could happen here in our small community."

"It's happenin' everywhere now, sis," he said. The sheriff took off his hat and rubbed his arm across his forehead. "And it's gonna get worse. There'll come a time when all of us will have to defend ourselves in our homes. We'd better be ready for it is all I can say."

Sarah thought it was an odd thing for the sheriff to say.

He was still surveying the property suspiciously. She tried to tell herself that he was simply worried about her, as he said. He could be deciding how safe he thought she was out here alone.

"Have they found anything?" she asked. "The van that the men were driving or—"

"No," the sheriff said. "Nothing yet. But we will," he said. "You can bet we'll find 'em, one way or another."

Sarah shivered. She supposed it was his job that made him sound so cold—after all, the sheriff saw violence on a regular basis.

But she couldn't forget that the man inside might be dead if he hadn't stumbled onto her porch. He could be lying in some ditch, covered by mud and water until someone found his cold, lifeless body.

Should she tell the sheriff about him?

"You sure you'll be all right out here alone?" he asked, as he turned to go.

"I'm sure," she said. "If I see anyone suspicious, I'll call your office."

"You do that," he said. He glanced over his shoulder and smiled rather fatherly at her. "In the meantime, keep your doors locked and don't let any strangers in under any circumstances. You still got that old shotgun your grand-dad used to have?"

Sarah shrugged her shoulders. "I'm sure it's here somewhere," she replied innocently.

"Might not be a bad idea to load it and keep it close by. Just till we get this whole thing settled. I'll give you a piece of advice, sis . . . though I'd have to deny sayin' it if it ever came up—if you see a stranger or someone trying to get into your house, you just shoot first and ask questions later."

She found his advice disconcerting, but she said nothing.

She thought he'd never leave. She'd been outside for quite a while now and she had a horrible vision of the stranger inside stumbling out on the front porch to find her.

She breathed a sigh of relief as she watched the sheriff open his car door. Then he stopped and turned, and came back toward her.

"Say, Sarah," he said, his gaze covering the empty driveway. "Where's that old pickup your granddad used to have? Red, wasn't it? I thought you started drivin' it when you moved out here."

Sarah swallowed hard and bit her lip.

"It's . . . it's in the shop. The old clunker is completely worn-out," she said. For the life of her she couldn't explain why she was lying. If she intended to tell him about the man who had stumbled onto her porch, now was the time.

"I took it in to have a tune-up and a few repairs done."

"That right?" he asked. "That's funny. I don't remember seein' it at Rainey's Garage today when I was there."

"Rainey's?" Sarah asked. She was practically holding her breath, hoping the sheriff wouldn't walk on out to the garage and peek in. "Oh, sure, Rainey's is where Granddad used to take it. No, I didn't take it there." Her mind was spinning as she tried to remain calm and sound as if she were telling the truth.

"Actually I took it to this guy over near Millwood. He's just a shade-tree mechanic, but someone told me he was very good and not quite so expensive as Rainey's."

"Ah," the sheriff said, nodding. "That explains it. So, I guess that wasn't you I saw in town last night. Thought I saw the old pickup on Central Ave."

"No," Sarah said, shrugging her shoulders. Central Avenue was near Lacy's house. Had he seen her last night...or was he just feeling her out? "It wasn't me," she lied.

"Guess you still don't get out much, huh?" he asked casually.

"No...I don't." At least that much wasn't a lie.

He nodded and glanced around once more before turning and moving back to the patrol car.

"You call me if you need anything now, you hear?" he asked as he stepped into the car. "And remember what I said about loadin' the shotgun."

"I will," Sarah said. "And thanks, Sheriff, for coming by to check on me."

The sheriff waved as he backed the car out of the driveway and turned back toward town.

Sarah walked toward the house and up onto the porch. She stood watching until the car was out of sight, then she sighed heavily and collapsed onto the top step.

"Oh, my God," she murmured. "It's just like grandmother always said, one lie just leads to another." She ran her hand over her face, then pushed her hair back and stood up.

She opened the front door quietly and tiptoed to the bedroom. The shades were drawn and the room where her patient slept was dim.

As she stepped into the room she was suddenly aware of someone beside her. She screamed and tried to move away just as his arm came out and grabbed her.

He pulled her against him, his breathing heavy and loud in the quiet room. His body was hot, burning with fever as he held her back against him and whispered against her ear.

"Did you call him while I was asleep? What did you tell him?" he hissed.

For a moment Sarah felt panic-stricken as she realized that she had trusted this man more than she should have. She'd been foolish enough to lie to protect him and in the process her only source of help had just driven away. She'd lied for a man who might very well be a cold-blooded killer.

"No, I didn't call him...and I didn't tell him anything," she said.

His arm was across her shoulders and neck as he held her tightly back against him.

"Don't lie to me..."

Sarah put her hand up to pull against his tensed forearm. She couldn't move her head to look at him.

"Please..." she said. She had to make him think she was calm and unfrightened. "Why are you doing this? I thought—"

"You thought I trusted you? Yeah, maybe I did," he growled. "And maybe that was a mistake. At this point I'd be a fool to trust anyone. Even someone as pretty as you."

"I swear to you—I didn't tell him anything."

"What did he want?" Hagan shook her a little for emphasis, but he didn't loosen his grip.

Sarah wondered how he managed to remain standing, much less hold her with such intensity. If the heat of his temperature was any indication, he was very, very sick.

"You're burning up," she said. She moved her head and tried to glance back at his face. "Let me help you back to bed and..."

That was a joke. He didn't seem to need any help. *She* was the one who needed help.

"Just answer my question," he growled.

Sarah sighed. Her hands were still on his arm and for a moment as she leaned against his hard body, she almost forgot that she was in danger.

"He mentioned the raid on the Satilla compound." She could feel his body tense as he listened. "He said the two men in the van hadn't been caught yet."

"What else?"

"He...he advised me to load Granddad's shotgun...and if anyone tries to break in, I should shoot first and ask questions later."

"That son of a bitch," he said in amazement. "He hopes you'll shoot me," his voice rasped. "Make the job easy for him."

Hagan grunted and leaned back against the wall, pulling Sarah with him.

"Do you really think he'd have driven away if I'd told him about you?" she asked.

"He might," he murmured.

"The van is probably in the river by now." Sarah had the feeling he was talking to himself more than to her. "This man came himself to see if my body was still in the ditch where they thought I'd be. And when it wasn't..." He grunted again.

Oddly, the same thought had crossed Sarah's mind. That was probably why, when the sheriff asked about her truck, she lied. Because she knew with a quiet, sinking feeling of fear, that he was involved in whatever had happened.

"He asked where my granddad's truck was and if I drove it last night," she said. Her voice was quiet and for a moment the room was completely silent.

"Oh, hell." He released her and turned her around to look at him, gripping her shoulders hard as he stared directly into her eyes.

"What did you tell him? Don't lie to me, Sarah." His brow was furrowed and Sarah thought she'd never seen anyone more intense— almost desperately so. "Because if you are..."

"I'm not lying," she said. "It's true that I've known Sheriff Metcalf all my life. But I don't trust him any more than you do. And I'm certainly not going to defend him if he's involved in this. I don't know how to convince you that I'm telling the truth."

"Why don't you trust him?"

"It's...it's personal," she said, not wanting to get into the story about the accident and Joe's work.

The man's jaw clenched and unclenched as he stared at her. As if he thought he could read her mind if he looked hard enough into her eyes.

She saw his white teeth biting at his lower lip and then he frowned. He seemed a bit confused and disoriented.

"Please," she said, reaching out. "You should be in bed. You're very weak and I'm afraid your fever has gone up even higher than before."

His knees buckled and then he caught himself and straightened. He pushed her hands away and walked stiffly and slowly toward the bed.

Sarah watched him with a mixture of disbelief and awe. What a stubborn man he was. He was too sick to walk and she could see for herself that he was in terrible pain. And yet he still wouldn't let her help him.

Once he was in bed, Sarah reached for the thermometer. Reading the numbers a few minutes later, she felt a sense of fear and despair wash over her.

What on earth was she doing trying to take care of someone as seriously ill as he was? He should be in a hospital with a critical-care doctor and twenty-four-hour nurses.

"We have to get your fever down," she murmured. "It's a hundred and three. I'm worried about this infection."

The man's eyes were bright. He hadn't stopped watching her the entire time.

"What . . . what did you tell him about the truck?" he asked, his breathing quick and hard.

Sarah sighed and shook her head. He wasn't going to rest or let the subject go until she'd told him everything he wanted to know.

"I told him it was being repaired."

He shook his head. "He won't believe that. All he has to do is send someone out here tonight when you're asleep. When he finds it, he's going to know you're lying. And he's going to know why."

"I can't help it," she said. "It was the only thing I could think of at the moment."

"It doesn't matter. I'm not saying you were wrong. I just wish to hell..."

"What?" she asked. "That you weren't here? That I wasn't involved? Well, I wish that, too. But you know, one thing I've learned this past year is that wishing really doesn't make it so. So I don't waste my time on wishes." She clamped her teeth together and stood up.

Hagan found his distrust diminishing as he stared at her.

When he looked into those blue eyes, he wished a lot of things. At the moment he wished he knew who he was and was strong enough to walk away from this place and this woman.

It was true he didn't like involving her, but there were other reasons for wanting to get away, too. Reasons he couldn't put a name to because they were pushed way down deep inside so far he couldn't even deal with them. He didn't have time for personal feelings right now. They only complicated things. And as he looked into Sarah's face, he sensed that she could complicate a man's life real good.

But the thing he wanted most had nothing to do with his instincts or survival, or even his memory. He found himself wanting to be the one to make that pain in her eyes disappear. He wanted to be the one to make her believe in wishes again. And those thoughts surprised and shook him.

Must be the fever.

Sarah turned away and left the room. When she returned she carried a washbasin and washcloth.

She pulled a chair beside the bed and pushed the covers away from him. She held a glass of water to his mouth and helped him swallow more tablets. Then, without a word, she pushed the robe away from his chest and began to bathe him in the cool water.

Hagan closed his eyes with a soft groan. He shivered and forced his eyes open again as he reached for the cloth.

"I can do that," he said through chattering teeth.

"No," Sarah said with a stubborn, haughty look. "I'm the nurse, you're the patient. Just lie still and let me do it."

He made no more protests, but Sarah thought it was only because he was too weak. She could feel his body shaking beneath her hands as she continued bathing him.

When he fell asleep she stopped. Somehow, asleep, he seemed too vulnerable for her to continue such an intimate act. Maybe it was her conscience. Maybe it was those erotic visions she'd had. Whatever it was she couldn't remember ever feeling that way before about any of her patients.

She sat watching him quietly, remembering how he had waited for her in the shadows and grabbed her when she came inside.

There was a fierceness in this man. Suspicion and cunning, and a fierceness that he probably kept masked by his outward charm.

Lawman or criminal . . . devil or angel. She couldn't decide.

She went into the kitchen and stood against the cabinet as she ate a piece of cheese and a slice of bread she had baked a couple of days ago. It tasted good to her. She hadn't realized how hungry she was or how tired.

Sarah knew she had to do something about the truck. If their suspicions about the sheriff were true, then it was only a matter of time until he learned the truck was here in her garage. And when he learned that Sarah had lied to him about it being repaired, he'd wonder why.

Sarah took the last bite of cheese and as she brushed the bread crumbs from her hands, she was already heading for the door.

It was late afternoon, but the sun still glistened brightly against the house and the tall grass out in the meadow. She probably should wait until dark, just in case someone was watching. But she really was afraid that might be too late.

The old garage was unique—her grandfather had built it with doors on both ends, so he could drive to or from the barn if he needed to. Sarah glanced toward the highway. If she drove the truck out the back of the garage, she thought she could manage to get it to the barn without anyone seeing her.

Hurriedly she went inside the garage, closing the front door and then going around the truck and her grandmother's old Buick to open the back doors. Her hands were trembling when she started the engine of the truck and drove it out the sandy road toward the barn.

She went around to the back of the barn, pulling into the wide opening that ran through the length of the building. Then twisting the steering wheel hard, she pulled the truck into one of the old stalls. It was one that hadn't been used in years, even when her grandfather still had livestock. It was filled with old harnesses and farm utensils, empty nail kegs and a half-empty barrel of tar that had been used to patch the barn roof.

Normally Sarah would take a moment to enjoy the familiar smells—even look around to see what treasure had been abandoned there—but today there was no time and she had too much to do. Looking at her watch, she knew she'd have to work quickly.

It took almost an hour and when she finished, Sarah was grimy and exhausted. She stood back and surveyed the stall. Now there was no trace of the truck, just a mound of hay filling the entire stall. She placed a couple of pitch-forks and a shovel against the front of the stack just to make it look authentic.

For a moment, as she stood looking at what she'd done, she wondered if she'd become completely paranoid. It seemed crazy. What if she'd done all this work for nothing? But, what if their suspicions were right? Then this would buy them a little time. Just until this man, whoever he was, was well and could leave her house.

She wished he had a name. She wanted to call him by his own name.

Sarah sneezed several times. The scent of hay was in her nostrils and her skin was covered with fine dust and debris from the dried grass.

Going back to the house, she went out the back of the barn. She used a piece of brush to rake back and forth across the road to obliterate any tire tracks she'd made in the dirt. Luckily it was sandy and the rain hadn't made it muddy.

She hurried into the garage and locked the back door. She glanced at the old Buick—she'd drive it if she needed to . . . if it still worked. She got into the dust-covered car, found the key over the sun visor and put it into the ignition.

She held her breath, breathing a sigh of relief when the engine cranked on the second try.

"Thank you . . . thank you," she whispered.

Then she ran back to the house. She'd have time to shower and change clothes, make a quick dinner.

First she tiptoed into the bedroom and placed her hand against her patient's forehead. He was still very hot, but she thought she detected just a hint of moistness on his skin.

She hoped his fever was about to break. He seemed to have no concept of how sick he was. And he kept his worries about the amnesia hidden. As for herself, she couldn't explain why she was going to all this trouble for a man she hardly knew. Or why she felt such an overwhelming need to protect him.

Chapter 6

After Sarah showered and changed into a pair of soft cotton shorts and shirt, she went to the kitchen to check on the soup she'd left simmering on the stove. She sliced more of the homemade bread and placed it with the soup and a glass of cool milk on a tray.

In the bedroom, she set the tray on the table beside the bed and stood for a moment, watching the stranger sleeping. She thought his breathing was still a little fast and shallow.

It was getting dark and the room was dim and shadowy. But she could see well enough to look at the bruises on his body. When she bathed him she had noticed other small scars and nicks on his skin and now she studied the telltale marks. Older scars. Garnered in the same violent way as the gunshot wound?

Sarah found herself longing to know more about him. She wanted to know all his secrets, all the hidden details that he couldn't or wouldn't remember.

She reached out and touched him. He was still hot and he needed nourishment. He had eaten very little these past few hours and she knew from experience that he would be susceptible to problems such as pneumonia for the next couple of days.

Her touch seemed to rouse him somewhat, although he didn't open his eyes. He kicked at the quilt and moved his head restlessly on the pillow.

"Are you awake?" she asked softly.

He opened his eyes and sighed heavily, then closed them again. She picked up his hand and it fell back onto the bed. His lethargic response sent a flicker of anxiety through Sarah and she knelt beside the bed and touched his face with the back of her hand.

"Can you hear me?" she said, more urgently. "You're scaring me. Don't you fade out on me now, you hear?" Sarah's breath came fast and hard as she ran her hands over his face and down his chest.

He muttered something unintelligible and continued moving his head back and forth.

"Come on," Sarah said again. She slapped his face lightly, sighing with pleasure when he opened his eyes and stared at her.

For once she was even delighted to see the anger snapping in those black depths.

"God," he murmured, scooting up in bed. "What kind of nurse are you, anyway? First you tie me up and now you hit me."

"I didn't hit you," she said, smiling despite herself. "I was afraid, that's all."

"Don't worry—I'm not about to die on you." He was staring at her oddly, and though his eyes were weak and tired, she thought there was a little flicker of humor there, too.

"Be quiet and let me take your temperature again." She pushed the thermometer between his lips.

"Sadistic," he muttered out of the side of his mouth.

She took the thermometer and nodded before putting it back in its case.

"Down a little. But not enough. I've brought something for you to eat. Can you manage?"

Sarah put her arm around his back, careful not to hurt his bruised ribs. Then as he braced himself and pushed upward, she slid the pillows behind him.

When he closed his eyes, she stood for a moment looking helplessly at him. He was very sick. Sicker than before? God, what if he died? What if he'd lost more blood than she thought, or developed a blood clot somewhere. It was improbable, but still, she found herself worrying about every remote dangerous possibility.

"Are you—?"

"I'm all right," he said with a touch of irritability. "Just a little dizzy, that's all."

"It's no wonder," she murmured.

He lifted his gaze toward her, staring at her with those fever-lit black eyes.

"You worry too much."

"I have a right to be worried about you," she said. She sat on the bed beside him, not caring what he thought. Not caring if he protested about her hovering. "I should go into town and try to get some antibiotics, but I can't leave you alone while you're so sick. Please..." She reached forward and placed her hand on his arm. "Please reconsider about the doctor—"

"Dammit, you just don't listen, do you?" He was breathing heavily and it seemed an effort for him to speak at all. "I don't want a doctor. I'll be fine. I've been in scrapes before and—" He stopped suddenly, realizing what he'd said.

"Do you remember something?" she asked breathlessly.

Hagan gritted his teeth as he tried to remember. Frowning, he lifted his hand and massaged his throbbing temple.

Sarah lifted her hand toward him, then thinking better of it, she stopped. She felt so helpless, so inadequate in the field of amnesia.

"It's as if there's something right on the tip of my tongue," he said. "You know? Like a dream you can't quite remember. And still, I can't make myself say it." He cursed quietly beneath his breath, his fists clenched against the bed. "Why can't I just say it, dammit?"

"Because you're sick and weak." She leaned forward to help with his dinner.

"No," he said, motioning her away. "Not until I remember . . . not until something . . ."

Sarah rolled her eyes with frustration. God, but he was stubborn.

"If pure obstinacy can make anyone well, I'm convinced you'll be healed in a matter of days."

"I don't have days," he snapped. "I have to get out of here. I need to know who this Cord guy is you said I mentioned. Right now it's all I have to go on." He glanced up at her intently, moving his legs as if he meant to get out of bed.

"Dear God." Sarah jumped up from the bed and crossed her arms as she stood staring at him. "You're unbelievable, do you know that? You have to be this missing agent. Your stubborn macho code certainly seems to fit the pattern."

"Yeah . . . right," he said, flashing her a look of determination. "Look," he said, his eyes cajoling a bit. "I'm fine. I'm just a little weak, that's all."

"Weak," she muttered, shaking her head. She turned and picked up the tray of food. "I'll believe you're fine when you've eaten all of your supper." She saw him grimace and she smiled. "Well, most of it, anyway."

As she bent and placed the food on his lap, she glanced down into his eyes. He was studying her intensely, letting his gaze wander over her scar, then linger on her mouth.

For a moment she couldn't breathe . . . or move. She was simply frozen by that look and by the electricity that tingled in the air between them.

When he reached up and touched her face, she flinched only the slightest bit, then stood stiffly as his finger traced the scar. His touch on the sensitive skin made her nerves tingle wildly. She jerked away from him and stood back from the bed.

As she looked into his eyes and saw his understanding, she felt stunned. No one had ever touched the scar. And it was the last thing she had expected from him.

He seemed so cool, so sophisticated and yet the look in his eyes was warm and filled with an unusual tenderness.

"You . . . you need to eat," she whispered.

She stood beside the bed, fists clenched. Her insides churned with emotion and made her wonder at her own sanity. How could she be feeling this way about a man she barely knew? A man who could be anything or anyone.

Then he smiled and turned his attention to the soup.

Sarah picked up the tray and hurriedly left the room.

In the kitchen, she wrapped her arms around her body, trying to still the heavy beating of her heart. God, she hoped he left soon. She didn't seem capable of controlling her emotions where he was concerned and she couldn't deny that she was attracted to him.

She liked touching him and she had to admit that her professional response often turned to something else once her hands touched his warm skin. His voice and the way he looked at her with those intense eyes made her tremble inside. And when he touched her...

"My...Lord..." she whispered, her breath coming in soft gasps.

"This is crazy," she said, turning to busy herself in the kitchen. She reminded herself again that she hardly knew this man. But it didn't seem to sink in.

There was an undeniable connection between them. Something she couldn't quite explain. Perhaps it had something to do with her rescuing him, saving his life. Perhaps it was the compassion she saw in his eyes when he looked at her and touched her scarred face without flinching or seeming to find her unattractive.

Or maybe it was that they both had been hurt in the past. And shared something as simple as pain and distrust of one's emotions.

She couldn't imagine what had made him wary and suspicious. At first glance he seemed to be a man who had it all. How ironic that neither of them knew for sure. What she did know was that he was tough and well conditioned. Proud. And she knew he was a survivor. And that a sense of humor sparkled in his eyes when he made light of himself and his injuries.

And there was an intense determination deep in those eyes. A dauntlessness that made her think she probably shouldn't be so worried about him after all. She even thought he might be one of those people who could will themselves to get well.

Still, there were so many questions remaining to be answered about him.

Just then she heard a noise in the bedroom. Feeling guilty she hurried into the hall and was met at the door by her patient who nodded curtly toward the bathroom.

She knew better than to try to help him, although he was so pale and weak he certainly seemed to need someone's help.

It was hard for Sarah as a nurse to stand by helplessly, without offering her assistance. But she sensed that this was his way of showing her that he was better and intended to get well without the aid of a doctor or anyone else.

She stood back and let him pass, watching him walk slowly, holding his arm tightly against his bruised side as he moved. Sweat beaded on his forehead, but Sarah wasn't sure if that was because his fever had broken, or because he was struggling so hard to walk.

Later when he came out of the bathroom he looked so ill that she couldn't keep from stepping forward.

"You look awful," she said.

"Thanks," he grunted. He walked with his right arm outstretched as he reached for the door frame and rested for a moment, breathing heavily. "God, I'm as weak as a baby."

"I don't know why you take that fact so personal," she said. "Anyone would be weak after what you've been through."

Sarah disregarded his murmur of protest and put her arm around him. She smiled to herself when this time he leaned heavily on her as they slowly made their way back to the bed.

As he sank back onto the bed, he closed his eyes briefly, then seemed to struggle to make himself alert.

"I have to get well...get away from here," he said. "For your own safety I have to get out of here. Your truck—"

"Don't worry about the truck," she said quietly. She touched his forehead and she thought he did feel a bit cooler. "I've taken care of it."

Hagan frowned at her. He had to fight the pain in his head and the effects of the sedative she'd given him earlier. He had to concentrate.

"I hid it in the barn and covered it with hay while you were sleeping this afternoon."

Hagan grunted humorously and shook his head.

"You're an amazing woman, Sarah James," he said. "Has anyone ever told you that?"

"Sure," she said, grinning. "Lots of times."

"Awhile ago...when you came inside from talking with the sheriff. I didn't mean to frighten you."

"You didn't."

"Yes...I did. I could hear it in your voice...you were beginning to have real doubts about me and I didn't make it any better."

"It's not that I don't trust you..."

He lifted his hand to stop her. "It's all right. I understand. I'd be worried if you weren't suspicious. Hell, I even thought you were one of them at first...one of my assassins, whoever the hell they are."

Sarah laughed at the thought.

"Do I look like an assassin?" she asked, spreading her arms and smiling wryly at him.

"No, ma'am," he said, his look amused. His eyes moved slowly from her face down past her breasts, to her hips and all the way down her bare legs. "Hardly that," he murmured, his voice warm with appreciation. When his gaze lifted again, he met her eyes and there was a burning curiosity behind his look. "You look like a very sweet, very caring and beautiful woman."

"You're delirious," she said, feigning lightheartedness. To be honest, his words and his soft, languid voice sent delicious shivers all the way down to her toes.

"I think your fever is down," she said. "But I'll wait awhile and take your temp again. I started my grandmother's old car earlier and it runs. So at least we have a vehicle now...in case we need it."

"That's good," Hagan said, pulling his gaze away from her.

He didn't know what the hell was wrong with him. He should be concentrating on getting himself out of this mess. Instead he found himself bantering flirtatiously with Sarah James, as if he had all the time in the world. He wanted to tease a smile to her sensuous lips. Wanted to see those beautiful eyes light just once with pleasure and joy. He knew he had made her uncomfortable just now when he looked at her. But it wasn't because she didn't welcome his attention. He remembered that much about women at least.

She was afraid to respond to him, he thought. And against his better judgment, he found that intriguing.

"I could use some clothes," he said. "I've been in this bed long enough."

Sarah didn't bother to disagree. Half a night and one day in bed was hardly enough for someone with so serious an injury. But she knew it was futile to tell him that. He was going to do what he wanted to do.

"Your suit's ruined," she said. "Although I might be able to salvage the pants."

"No," he said. "Burn it."

"What? But the suit must have cost a fortune. Probably as much as I make working at the hospital in a month."

"Burn it." He glanced down at the old flannel robe he was wearing. "Whose is this? Your grandfather's?"

"Yes."

"Don't you have any more of his clothes somewhere?"

"Well, yes," she said, smiling. "But he was a much bigger man than you...rounder, anyway. I don't think..."

"Anything will do."

"I could go into town...pick up something for you there," she offered.

"Are you in the habit of buying men's clothes?" His eyes sparkled when he asked the question. "Any particular man, that is?"

"No," she said, shaking her head. "There's no man. I'll find something here for you tomorrow if you still think you want to get up, but considering the clothes you were wearing, I doubt you're going to like them."

"I'll like anything," he said. "As long as I can get out of this bed."

She didn't doubt it. And she certainly didn't doubt his determination anymore. He didn't complain much and she wasn't sure how he stood the pain; she knew the medication she'd given him wasn't strong enough.

Hagan watched Sarah. He had a hunch she'd already had enough problems in her life without becoming embroiled in this kind of business. But he needed her. And he was going to have to trust her.

That might be a harder task. He also had a hunch that he wasn't used to trusting anyone.

His head was hurting again and there were flashes of light and words, pieces of conversation all jumbled together inside his brain.

Suddenly his eyes widened with a spark of excitement.

"Get a pencil," he said, motioning toward Sarah. "Quick...write this down."

Sarah looked at him oddly, but she did as he asked, rummaging in the table beside the bed for a pencil and piece of paper.

He said the numbers quickly, as if he was afraid he might forget before she could write them down.

"I got it," she murmured. She read the numbers back to him. "Not enough for a social security number," she said. "Seven numbers . . . I think it's a phone number."

"I think it is, too." Hagan rubbed his head, trying to remember and feeling frustrated that the number just came from nowhere, with nothing to connect it to a person or place.

"It's not a local number. Heck," she muttered. "It could be anywhere in the country."

"No, it's in Georgia," he said thoughtfully. "Am I still in Georgia?"

"Yes, you are," she whispered. "You're remembering."

"We have to call this number. Where's a phone? Do you have a portable?" he asked, looking around the room.

"Are you kidding?" she laughed. "My grandfather thought it was sinful just having two regular old-fashioned dial phones in the house."

Her patient grinned at her. When he looked that way, Sarah wondered how she could ever suspect him of being a criminal. He looked like nothing more than a handsome, flirtatious man with a winning smile and enough charisma to run for office.

"There's a phone in the hall and one in the kitchen . . . if you can make it."

"I can make it," he said through gritted teeth. There was a definite lift in his voice now and Sarah hoped for his sake that this phone number led to something concrete.

He swung his legs over the side of the bed, hesitating only a moment before pulling the old robe together and standing.

His actions reminded Sarah that he was completely naked beneath the robe. And for a moment she couldn't seem to make herself think of anything else.

She went into the hallway and dialed the phone while he went to the kitchen table with the other phone in front of him. She could see his body shaking from the effort, even from where she stood.

It seemed an eternity before the phone began to ring on the other end. She nodded to her patient and he picked up his phone, staring down the hall at her.

"Georgia Bureau of Investigation," the voice on the phone said. "How may I direct your call?"

If her mystery man was surprised, he didn't show it. In fact, he was cool...almost too cool as he hung up his phone and motioned for Sarah to do the same. She couldn't keep the tremor out of her voice when she spoke.

"I...I'm sorry," she stammered. "I'm afraid I've dialed the wrong number." She hung up the phone and went into the kitchen, sitting down at the table across from him.

"Why did you hang up?" she asked. "Why didn't you ask about this missing agent? If they could send us a picture of him or—"

Hagan leaned his head to one side and laughed, his eyes sparkling at her.

"Yeah, sure. They're not releasing any info to the public, so they're not about to tell some stranger on the phone about this guy." His eyes grew serious and he rubbed his chin thoughtfully.

"I have to think," he murmured, almost to himself.

"How about doing that back in bed?" she suggested softly. "You're very pale and you're shaking."

"I'm not shaking," he growled.

"Trust me, you're shaking," she said, looking at him as if she were his teacher.

"You don't leave me much choice about this, do you?" he said, grunting humorously. "I'm kind of at your mercy here, aren't I?"

"Yes . . . you are," she said, meeting his gaze.

"All right," he said, standing up.

"Well, finally," she said. "That's more like it."

"Turnabout's fair play," he said, shrugging. "I trust you and you trust me."

Why did she get the feeling he was asking her a question with that last phrase? Was he testing her? Like a little boy, was he trying to see how far he could go and how much she cared?

"My granddad used to have a saying," she said. "I'll trust any man until he gives me a reason not to trust him."

He looked into her eyes.

"Sounds like a very wise man," he murmured.

"Yes . . . he was."

Hagan found himself wanting to thank her for all she'd done. But where Sarah James was concerned, he found that he was feeling other needs as well, much more compelling needs. And much more troubling.

After he was settled in bed and Sarah had left, Hagan lay alone thinking and listening to the silence of the old house. It went against every instinct he had to lie helplessly while someone else waited on him. And it galled him that he wasn't able to offer much help or protection to Sarah. Hell, at this point he could hardly even protect himself.

He was weak and his side ached. Sometimes the pain was so unbearable that it made him as irritable as a bear. But he could handle that part. What he was finding intolerable was the weakness, the inability to do even the smallest tasks for himself.

And there was Sarah. Sweet, compassionate Sarah with those big vulnerable blue eyes.

He was beginning to notice a feeling of peace when she came into the room. If he'd had a happy home as a child, he might equate it with that feeling. But that was something he didn't know. Whatever it was, he found it hard to explain and he could only blame it on his weakened condition and the fact that he had come so close to dying.

His thoughts went back to Sarah. She was beautiful, there was no denying that. Even the scar couldn't take away her beauty. She had a clear-eyed healthy look about her, her dark hair heavy and thick and shining with warm auburn highlights. And although she was petite, there was a womanly softness about her, with rounded hips and breasts. She was the kind of woman who made a man feel completely male.

"Damn," he muttered.

He hardly knew this woman and yet the images of her were already becoming all too familiar. Even now he could feel the touch of her hands, gentle and nurturing as she tended him. He was certain he'd even been aware of her hands in his fevered sleep.

That haunting rose scent seemed to linger in the room long after she was gone. Warm and sweet and surprisingly erotic.

Hagan cleared his throat and shifted his weight in bed.

When she'd come in after talking with the sheriff and he had confronted her, he'd seen the spark of fear leap to her eyes. Yet later when he touched her scar she hadn't pulled away.

She shouldn't trust so easily. And she probably shouldn't trust him at all.

The scar on her face had felt soft, not much different than the rest of her skin, except for the rippled texture. And he had found himself wanting to hold her, to kiss that ragged mark and tell her that everything was going to be all right.

But he didn't have the right to do any of those things.

Was she the kind of woman he was usually attracted to? Hell, he couldn't even be sure about something so simple as that. He had a gut feeling he wasn't married, and that there was no special woman in his life. He thought he'd know somewhere in the back of his mind if he were in love with a woman.

But had he ever been married?

Was that why being here with her gave him such a sense of peace? Why he enjoyed her taking care of him so much? Maybe it was that sense of marriage, of belonging somewhere, to someone, that made him feel so good when she was near.

Sarah was efficient and caring. He'd watched her work and seen how organized and logical she was about things. Her clothes were neat but simple and he'd noticed that she wore the same tiny gold earrings all the time, and very little, if any, makeup.

He gazed around the old-fashioned shabby room. How many of the women he'd known would even be caught dead in a place like this?

But the house obviously meant something to Sarah.

Sentiment.

He'd be willing to bet that was another thing he hadn't had much room for in his life.

"No way I'm going to start now," he muttered before drifting off to sleep.

Chapter 7

It was late when Hagan woke. He lay for a moment, feeling an unsettling sense of being in a strange house without knowing where or who he was.

He turned his head and saw Sarah sitting in the rocker, reading. She looked so normal and so reassuring.

When she looked up at him and smiled, that odd feeling of peace swept over him and he closed his eyes again. Almost immediately he felt his pulse slow as he took another good, deep breath of air.

"While you were sleeping I thought of something," Sarah said, scooting forward in her chair.

"What?" he asked, his voice still drowsy.

"What if we call the number again and ask for Cord?"

The room was very quiet. For a second Sarah practically held her breath as she stared into his eyes.

"I don't know why I didn't think of that," he said. "It's worth a try."

Sarah stood back when he got out of bed, not attempting to help him this time.

They went back to their same positions, he at the kitchen table and she at the phone in the hall. Sarah dialed the number.

The operator answered the phone the same as before.

"May I speak to Cord please?" Sarah asked.

"Cord?" the operator asked.

"I...yes, I only have his first name. Is there anyone there with that—"

"Just a moment please."

Sarah glanced toward the kitchen. She could hear his soft breathing through the phone. Looking into his eyes suddenly made her feel strange, almost as if he were touching her from there.

"Hello?"

The deep male voice that came on the phone made Sarah jump. She was so surprised that for a moment she couldn't speak. Her mouth worked, but no words came. She glanced helplessly toward the man in the kitchen, seeing the puzzled expression on his face as well, and motioning for him to speak.

"Cord?" he asked.

Sarah held her breath. She could hear the odd blending of hope and uncertainty in his voice.

"Yes," the man named Cord answered slowly. "Who's this?"

"It's me, buddy," Hagan said.

"Hagan? My God, Hag, is that you?" The man's voice suddenly became lower, more secretive.

"Does it sound like me?"

Sarah watched the man at the table shrug his shoulder and smile sheepishly at her. She was transfixed, watching and listening to this odd conversation.

"Where are you?" Cord demanded. "Are you all right? God, man, do you know how hard we've all been looking for you? Why haven't you tried to get in touch with us before now?"

Suddenly Hagan hung up the phone. But Sarah's line was still open. She could hear the man named Cord on the other end of the phone.

"Hello? Hagan? Hagan?" Then curses as the phone went dead.

Sarah hung up and hurried to the kitchen.

"You're him," she whispered. "You're this agent they're looking for. He recognized your voice. Why on earth did you hang up?"

Her patient was shaking and perspiration stood out on his neck and face.

"How do I know I can trust this man when I don't even remember who the hell he is? Someone betrayed me. For all I know, it could have been him."

"You're right," Sarah said, sliding into a chair. "Okay." She held her hands up, nodding slowly as she tried to think rationally. "We just have to think this through."

"Hell, I don't even know what to ask him," he said.

"I know." Impulsively Sarah reached across the table, touching his hand. "It must be awful, not knowing who you are...who you can trust."

"I trust you," he said. "Right now, all I know is that I trust you, Sarah. And even that makes me feel pretty damn guilty."

"Well, it shouldn't," she said, looking into his eyes. "Don't feel guilty about me. I wouldn't be doing this if I didn't want to."

"I'm helpless here, dammit."

"Frankly, I think you're about as helpless as a bulldozer," she said, smiling.

Just then the phone rang, shattering their conversation and causing Sarah to jump. He motioned her to answer.

"Hello?" She frowned as she stared into her patient's eyes. "Who is this?" the deep voice demanded. "Someone there just called the G.B.I. office in Atlanta." He sounded angry and he sounded like a man who tolerated little nonsense.

"Cord?" she asked, her eyes growing wide.

The man across the table from her frowned and shook his head.

"How...how did you know?" she asked.

"The line's not tapped if that's what you're worried about. Just tell me, dammit, who it was who called me from there."

"I...I think I need to know a little more about you first," she said, ignoring her patient's look of warning. "We're not sure at this point who to trust and who—"

"Let me speak to Hagan," Cord demanded.

Sarah swallowed hard. She was caught between the two men, and taking charge of the situation was not an easy thing for her to do.

"You see...the problem is," she began slowly. "We...he's not sure who he is—"

"Not sure who he is? What the hell do you—"

"He has amnesia," she said quickly.

There was a long pause on the other end of the phone.

"Hang up." Hagan reached for the phone, his look dark with caution. But Sarah swung away from him, frowning and mouthing her answer toward him.

"No."

"If you can just tell me something about him," Sarah said into the phone. "Something to let me know it's really him. And something about yourself, maybe."

"Look," Cord said, his voice deep and steady. "We're partners. We've been best friends since we began working together ten years ago. He was the best man at my wedding a couple of weeks ago." He stopped, muttering beneath his breath as he tried to think of other things to tell her.

"He says you're best friends," she said. "And that you were best man at his wedding a couple of weeks ago."

Hagan frowned, trying to remember. The name Cord sounded more and more familiar, but he still couldn't put a face to the name.

"Is he hurt?" Cord asked. "You can tell me that at least, can't you?"

"He has a graze to the head where a bullet barely missed sending him to the morgue," she said, watching Hagan. "Possible cracked ribs and an infection—I'm not sure if it's from the bullet wound or all the swamp water he swallowed. But he's so stubborn he won't let me call a doctor."

Cord laughed softly.

"He can be as stubborn as a mule."

Sarah smiled.

Cord cared about this man sitting across from her. She could hear it in his voice and it was what finally convinced her they should trust him.

"What does he look like?" she asked, grinning at Hagan's look of exasperation. She knew he hated every minute of this and that he would be much happier grabbing the phone and taking care of everything for himself. But at the moment she thought she was the better judge of the truth.

"Medium height," Cord said. "He's wiry, with muscular shoulders and chest. Dark skin . . . brown hair, kind of bleached out by the sun—from playing tennis." Then he chuckled again. "Eyes blacker'n sin."

Sarah tilted her head back and laughed aloud, then explained to a curious Hagan.

"He says your eyes are blacker than sin."

"He likes expensive clothes," Cord continued. "Kind of a modern-day Beau Brummell. Damn, I wish I could remember the name of some of the stuff he wears, but..."

"Gucci shoes? Tino Cosma ties?" Sarah smiled at the look on Hagan's face.

"Yeah," Cord said. "Yeah, that sounds right."

"I think you've definitely convinced me it's him," Sarah said. "Now all you have to do is convince him."

"Tell him he's a Georgia Tech runt," Cord said.

"What?"

"Just tell him."

Sarah shrugged apologetically and repeated Cord's words.

"You tell him I can whip his redneck Bulldog ass any day of the year," Hagan snapped.

He had said the words without thinking. And now he shook his head and laughed as a look of wonder crossed his handsome face.

Sarah didn't have to relay anything to Cord. He had heard it and was laughing aloud. And there was a noted sound of relief in his voice.

"That's him, all right," he declared. "Put him on the phone."

Grinning, Sarah handed the phone to Hagan. He had a name. Now she knew what to call him and she didn't have to be afraid anymore.

At least she didn't have to worry that he was a criminal. Looking into his dangerous eyes, she thought there might be other things she should be afraid of.

"Yeah?" Hagan said.

"Hagan Cantrell, you dog."

"Jeez, with all these insults, I'm beginning to wonder about this friendship you say we're supposed to have," Hagan drawled.

Cord laughed, then grew more serious.

"It's good to hear your voice. I thought you were a goner for sure. I was afraid they'd dumped your body in the swamp where we'd never find you."

"I think that was the plan," Hagan said. "Not that I can remember it yet. So...we're partners?"

"For ten years," Cord said. "Don't you remember any of it?"

"Nothing," Hagan said. "I feel as if I've fallen into a big black hole somewhere. Say, if we're partners, why weren't you down here with me on this case?"

"I was on my honeymoon...a fact I'm sure you're never going to let me forget when this is all over."

Hagan laughed. His dark eyes crinkled at the corners and the sound of his laughter rumbled up from his chest to fill the room with its deep, joyful sound. He bent slightly, holding his bruised side as he laughed.

Sarah caught her breath and put her hands up to her mouth. It was the first time he'd laughed that way—fully and with no holding back. And the sound, the look on his face, actually took her breath away. Oddly she felt hot tears stinging her eyes.

Hagan looked into Sarah's eyes and frowned just as she stood up and began to clean an already spotless countertop.

She was aware of Hagan's conversation with Cord as he told how he hadn't wanted her to call the sheriff. How Sarah was a nurse.

When she sensed his gaze on her, she didn't turn around. There was too much she was feeling at the moment. She was happy for him, of course, but there was a fear in her, too. And she had the oddest feeling of pain and loneliness, as if she were about to lose something very precious.

"Her name is Sarah James," she heard him say. Then to her, "Sarah . . . what's the address here?"

She turned then and gave him the address. Her hands were behind her as she steadied herself against the kitchen counter.

He repeated the address to Cord and then hung up the phone.

"He'll be here in the morning," he said.

"That's good," she whispered. "Wonderful . . . I'm so happy for you." She chided herself silently when her voice caught and reflected the anguish she felt.

Hagan stood up and came slowly toward her, not taking his eyes from her face.

"Sarah . . ." he murmured. "What's wrong? I'd have thought this was what you wanted." He took her shoulders, running his hands lightly down her arms as he looked into her eyes.

"A least you don't have to be afraid anymore. You know I'm not a criminal. Although quite honestly, you might be in more danger from a federal officer . . ." His eyes sparkled as he tried to tease her out of her sadness.

"How do you feel about all this?" she asked lightly. "Are you relieved . . . did he help you remember anything else?"

"Don't change the subject," he said. "We're talking about you now. While I was on the phone there were tears in your eyes. And I want to know why."

Sarah shook away his words, trying to smile convincingly.

"I'm just . . . I'm happy for you, that's all."

She glanced up from beneath her lashes, meeting his eyes and feeling a spark of electricity travel from where his hands touched her, all the way down to her toes.

It seemed an eternity that they stood there, staring into each other's eyes. Sarah wasn't sure how their bodies suddenly became so close, touching almost. Or when the sparks between them caught and blazed into open sexual awareness.

But suddenly she was conscious of him as she'd never been of any other man. She was aware of sensations she'd thought were lost to her forever.

His fingers burned her skin and his dark gaze wouldn't let her go. And his mouth. The fact that it was only mere inches from capturing hers sent her head reeling.

She was the one to break that last small boundary between them.

The one who moved, ever so slightly toward him.

She heard the whisper of her name, then his muffled groan and the rough, erotic feel of his hands in her hair. His kiss was electric and intense, just the way she had imagined. Her mouth opened for him and she thrilled to the erotic taste of his tongue and the rough texture of his unshaven skin. The kiss seemed to explode between them into a moment of unbearable heated passion, one neither of them could stop or temper. As if they had been waiting for this moment their entire lives.

Sarah moved against him, moaning as her hands moved inside the robe to the mat of hair on his chest. How could she, in her wildest dreams, have thought she could live without this? Without him?

She had never been so achingly aware of a man's body, or so ready for his possession as she was at that moment. She didn't care about anything except the touch of his hands, his mouth. If he had told her right then and there that he was indeed a criminal, a murderer even, she thought she still couldn't have made herself stop.

Hagan's hands were on her hips, pulling her against him, letting her feel the heat of his hard body against hers. As their mouths clung hungrily, Sarah could feel their bodies shaking. They were so close that she couldn't tell if the trembling came from her or from him.

"Sarah," he whispered. "Sweet little Sarah." His mouth pulled at her bottom lip, then slipped to the corner of her mouth and the edge of the scar.

Sarah jerked away, staring up at him and into those dark fathomless eyes. Eyes that urged her to relent, eyes that were tender and sweet. Patient. And as dangerous as any she'd ever looked into.

When he pulled her toward him again, she didn't protest, but closed her eyes as he kissed the scar. She wasn't sure how he managed to turn what she expected to be a disturbing moment into something more...into a moving, deeply erotic sensation.

She felt her knees buckle and she had to hold on to him to keep from falling.

His hands touched her everywhere, moving over her with an expertise that left her trembling and wanting more. Until she felt herself burning with a passion she knew she'd never experienced before.

Not even with her lost husband.

"No," she managed to say, pulling away from his seeking mouth. "Wait..." The horror and deceitfulness of her thoughts struck her like a fist.

He was staring at her with those mysterious black eyes. Watching her warily with just a touch of humor that never quite reached past the corner of his lips.

But he relented, stepping back and holding his hands up as one might do when trying to calm a shy colt.

"I . . . I can't do this," she said, still gasping for air.

"Why not?" he whispered.

One hand reached out to cup her face and without thinking she leaned into it, breathing the scent of his skin, reveling in the warmth and strength of his palm.

"Please," she pleaded, opening her eyes. "I just can't."

"I don't want you to do anything you don't want to do," he said. But his hoarse, emotion-filled voice belied his words. "I thought—"

"I know," she said, her eyes filled with apology. "I know what you must think and I'm sorry. I just can't let myself—"

"Why, Sarah?" he asked again.

She shook her head. She couldn't think when he was so near. And she couldn't explain how or why she was feeling such sorrow . . . such guilt. Except that this man, this stranger, had made her feel overwhelming emotions in mere minutes, that she had never experienced with Joe in their lifetime.

"I hardly know you," she whispered, her stricken eyes staring into his. But it wasn't that and she knew it. It was Joe. . .and the terrible guilt she felt. As if he were still alive and right there in the room beside her. Watching her with accusing, pain-filled eyes.

"You know me," Hagan said, his voice steady.

"I . . . I'm not the kind of woman to . . . to—"

"I know you're not, dammit," he said. "You don't have to tell me that."

He moved only a fraction of an inch toward her and yet even that tiny step closer made her heart beat erratically.

"Tomorrow you'll be gone," she said. "Just like the storm . . . like the cat." Sarah waved her hands ineffectually, feeling foolish as she saw the faint smile on his lips and the humorous lift of his brow.

"The cat?" he asked wryly.

"A stray tabby who came here a few months ago. Every time I'd begin to get used to him, he'd leave," she continued, not knowing why. "I would wake up one morning and he'd just be gone. And each time I thought he'd never come back."

He nodded, understanding her comparison now. He was smiling, yet his eyes still stalked her hotly.

"But he did come back," he said.

"Yes . . . but . . ."

"He's here now, isn't he?" he said. "The cat?" His voice was completely calm and practical, different than it had been only moments before.

"But not to stay," she whispered. "I don't think he has it in him to stay in one place forever . . . with one person."

"I see," he said. "And that's what you think of me. Here today . . . gone tomorrow?"

"You can't deny that."

"Only because I don't remember," he said.

Hagan pulled away, putting distance between him and her soft, tempting body. "But you're right. I don't know what kind of man I am. But like you I have a feeling I'm probably not the kind to stick around for long."

Sarah held herself very still.

He let his eyes move over her quickly, regretfully.

"If that's what you want, darlin' . . . then I'm sorry."

Chapter 8

Hours later Sarah was lying in bed. Still awake. Still trying to keep the images out of her head. Trying to banish the sensations that raced through her when she thought of his mouth on hers, the touch of his body against hers. A man she hardly knew...a stranger who had come to her home without a name and still without a past.

But he had a name now. Hagan. Hagan Cantrell. She had let the sound of it linger in her mind, had whispered the name aloud to see how it felt on her tongue.

A stranger no longer. Not after today.

She had responded to his touch as if she'd known him forever. As if making love to him would be the most natural thing in the world.

So easy, her mind whispered.

"And so crazy," she replied.

She kicked the sheets restlessly and slid out of bed, going to the window for what seemed to be the thousandth time.

She was tired and all she really wanted was to sleep.

But she couldn't.

She had thought she would feel such relief if she only knew he wasn't a criminal. That he wasn't one of those wild-eyed men in camouflage, whose minds were filled with paranoia. She hadn't wanted him to be one of those men.

Was it any better now that she knew he was a G.B.I. agent? This was a man who lived life on the edge even if he did maintain an outward appearance of cool indifference to life's horrors.

He was a loner. A man who probably chose not to have a family because of his work. Or because he didn't trust the violent world he lived in.

As foolish as it had sounded, she hadn't been far from the mark when she compared him to her wandering Tom.

She shook her head and walked back to the bed, determined to concentrate on sleep. Instead she found her thoughts again straying, wandering to the vision of Hagan as he'd been in bed that first night . . . before she knew him . . . before she had looked into those mesmerizing eyes.

And his mouth. Whether he was frowning or smiling, those deep grooves beside his mouth fascinated her.

How many times during first few hours had she toyed with the idea of kissing him? How many times had she secretly wondered how it would feel . . . how he would taste?

And now she knew.

Sarah gasped and sat up in bed. She could feel the electricity tingling in every inch of her body. The mere thought of him lying in the room next door was enough to take her breath away.

"You have to stop this," she muttered, shaking her head.

It was long past midnight before Sarah finally drifted off to sleep. She woke the next morning to the sound of water running and for a moment she couldn't identify where it was coming from.

She grabbed a robe and stepped to the door. Looking across the hall she could see the bathroom door open. Only a portion of Hagan's body was visible as he stood before the small vanity, shaving.

Sarah stepped quietly across the hall, noting the pleasant, self-absorbed look on Hagan's face. Obviously he hadn't spent a miserable night as she had, tossing and turning. It seemed obvious that what had happened between them had not disturbed him half as much as it had her.

That thought irritated her to no end.

Hagan turned, still holding the razor in his hand as he stared at her. His eyes moved from her tousled hair down over her breasts and hips to where the silky wrap stopped above her knees.

"I borrowed your granddad's old razor," he said, turning it in his hands. "I hope you don't mind."

"Of course I don't mind," she said. "You must be feeling better."

"Much better," he said, bringing his gaze up to her eyes. "How about you?"

"Me?" she asked, shrugging as if she didn't know what he meant. "I'm fine. Just fine. Your partner should be here soon, shouldn't he? Are you nervous?"

"Anxious," he murmured, twisting his mouth as he shaved. "I've tried to remember what he looks like." He shrugged his shoulders, his look one of frustration.

"Sometimes seeing someone or something will trigger a memory," she said.

"I know...like seeing your granddad's shotgun made me remember about guns."

"Exactly." Her eyes touched briefly on his chest, seen through the opening of the robe. She found herself longing to know what he would look like in real clothes. "Would you like some coffee?"

"I'd love some coffee," he said.

"You seem..."

"What?" he asked.

After laying down the razor, he took a towel and wiped the rest of the shaving soap off his face.

He was a beautiful man.

The clean scent of him seemed to move out and wrap around her as she stood staring at his smooth face. What was it about a man's freshly shaven face that made a woman want to touch it? To nuzzle against it?

"Sarah?" he reminded.

"Oh...sorry. I guess I'm not quite awake this morning. I just thought you seemed happier somehow this morning. Have you remembered anything new?"

"No," he said, shaking his head. "But I'm hopeful. And at least now I know who I'm not."

"Yes," she agreed. "That must be a relief."

Hagan looked into her tired eyes. Where was this small talk going? Was she feeling awkward about what had happened between them last night? Was he fighting this tingle of electricity that arced between them even now, just as hard as she was?

Hagan stepped out into the hallway, noting the look of alarm on Sarah's face as he came closer to her. Without speaking he reached out and took her left hand, letting his fingers rub the soft flesh of her ring finger.

"Does this small mark on your finger have something to do with why you're so reluctant to become involved with

a man? Or should I take what happened last night personally and consider that I'm the problem?''

His deep, slow drawl drew her closer. Sarah felt her
mouth grow dry and she licked her lips self-consciously.

''I . . . I don't know what you mean,'' she answered.

Hagan held her hand up between them.

''There was once a ring here,'' he said. ''Right where the
white circle is and this tiny indentation. You must have
worn it for a long time.''

Sarah pulled her hand away and took a step away from
him. She might have removed her wedding ring a year ago,
but its presence could still be seen, just as it still was felt in
her heart. She'd taken off that ring the day of Joe's fu-
neral and placed it on his little finger to be buried with
him.

Her eyes, when they met Hagan's again, were troubled
and filled with a pain that she could not quite manage to
hide.

''You're very observant,'' she said, her voice a mere
whisper. ''I suppose that's part of your job.''

''Maybe,'' he said, his gaze cutting her no slack.

''I was married,'' she said softly.

''He left you.'' Hagan nodded, with a knowing lift of his
brow. ''And now you're afraid to let anyone else get close
enough to hurt you again.''

Sarah's eyes sparkled and her lips pressed tightly together.

''Well, you're quite an armchair psychiatrist, aren't
you? I hate to disappoint you, but I'm afraid you're way
off the mark on your diagnosis, Doctor.''

Hagan's lifted his brows and a slight grimace tugged at
the corner of his mouth.

''Evidently not too far,'' he said. ''If what I said upsets
you so much.''

"I'm not upset," she snapped, turning to go toward the kitchen.

"Sarah." Hagan's hand reached out, catching her arm and turning her back to face him. He held her there, determined that this time she wasn't going to run from him. Or this conversation. "Just tell me what it is."

"Why?" she asked. "Does it bother you so much for a woman to tell you no?"

Hagan's head turned to one side and he frowned. But still he didn't release her, or step away from her.

"Well, now, I really can't answer that, can I?" he drawled. "All I have to go on is how I feel right now. And right now, yes, it does bother me. What's the big deal?" He shrugged his broad shoulders.

"My husband is dead." She blurted the words out in one harsh jumbled rush. "That's the big deal...okay?" She jerked away from him and headed toward the kitchen.

Hagan's mouth was open as he stood watching her go. He took a deep gulp of air, feeling as if he'd just been kicked in the stomach. Why hadn't he thought of that? Why hadn't he realized it? All the signs were there. That quiet look of hurt in her eyes...the scar on her face, the way this house didn't seem to fit with his image of her. He'd seen for himself that she was a caring, efficient nurse. Yet she wasn't practicing what she'd been trained for. Hell, that was probably the biggest giveaway of all.

He could see her in the kitchen, quietly opening the cupboards, setting out cups and coffee creamer. Hagan closed his eyes and shook his head, then raked his hand down his face.

He must have sounded like the biggest jerk in the world.

Slowly he walked into the kitchen. He saw Sarah turn just slightly toward the entryway, then go back to what she was doing with her back to him.

He leaned against the wide arched door frame.

"I should have known... It was the car accident." His voice was soft...searching. "The same one where you got the scar."

Sarah nodded, but she didn't turn to face him. She placed the filter and coffee in the basket, then poured the water into the coffeemaker. Still she didn't turn around.

"It was more than a year ago," she murmured. "Everyone says I should be over it by now. They probably think I'm crazy for continuing to live out here alone, like some kind of hermit."

"You're not crazy," he said. "You're the sanest person I know." He laughed softly. "But then, hey... you're the *only* person I know."

Sarah's laugh sounded more like a sob. She caught herself against the counter, head bent. When she finally turned to face him, there were tears sparkling in her eyes.

"I didn't mean to hurt you by being so insensitive," he said. "I'm sorry... really sorry."

Sarah's chin trembled. She blinked her eyes against the pain in her chest, trying to push away the tears. Her entire body trembled from the effort.

"Hey," he said softly.

With two steps, he was there, taking her into his arms, and holding her against him as the sobs came. His hand cradled her head against his chest as he murmured soft words against her hair.

Sarah made protests, quietly chiding herself for her weakness. But his sweet words and the look of sympathy in his eyes turned her legs to jelly and she didn't seem to have any control left.

"It's all right to cry," he said, holding her tightly. "God knows if anyone deserves a good cry, you do. Sometimes I wish I could cry—hell I haven't cried since I was..."

Sarah felt his body stiffen and she pulled back. She was no longer thinking of herself or her loss, but of him and the odd, puzzled look in his eyes.

"When?" she asked gently. "Tell me when the last time was."

"I was twelve," he said blankly. Holding his sore ribs, Hagan moved away from her and carefully slid onto one of the kitchen chairs. There was an air of expectation about him, a quiet look of wonder on his face as if he were a child trying to recite a memorized poem.

Sarah waited breathlessly.

"My mother was angry because I'd barged into the apartment. She had a visitor." Hagan's lips curled with disdain, but still he kept staring into space.

"She had a lot of visitors," he said quietly. "And a lot of them were drunk. But this one was an ugly drunk...and mean." Hagan frowned and clenched his teeth together.

Sarah wanted to go to him. To touch him...hold him while he remembered this thing that was so obviously painful to him. But she didn't dare break the spell for fear his memories would shatter and disappear.

"Did...did he hit you?" she said, her voice a bare whisper.

"No," he answered grimly. "It wasn't that." When he lifted his head, his eyes were glittering and hard. "He asked if I wanted to join them, if I wanted them to teach me... My mother just laughed...and I ran. I guess that was the last day I ever spent in that place."

"Oh, Hagan..." she whispered. Tears filled her eyes and she took a step toward him. "Oh..." she sighed, feeling the tears mark their hot path down her cheeks.

She thought for a moment that he was near tears, too. But then with a lift of his brow, he stood up. She could see his clenched jaw and the hard look in his eyes.

"Well hell," he said, shrugging his broad shoulders. "No wonder I didn't want to remember anything, huh?" His laugh was harsh and forced.

She wiped away her tears. "Has it all come back?" she asked, knowing that it sometimes happened that way with amnesiacs.

"No," he snapped. "Not all of it...just the good parts."

"Hagan," she murmured. "Don't do this. Let me fix you some breakfast. I'll—"

"Sorry, but I seem to have lost my appetite." His reply was brusque, with that hint of irritability she'd seen before.

He didn't look at her again as he pushed himself away from the table and took a slow step into the hallway.

"I need to walk a little. If I stay in that bed one more minute..." He gritted his teeth and glanced around at her. "Do you mind if I look around?" he asked, nodding toward the rest of the house.

"No, go ahead," she murmured. She still had to fight the impulse to touch him, to put her hand on his arm and comfort him. Instead, she waved her hand toward the tiny house. And when he moved away, she didn't follow.

Hagan stopped at the room just next to his and pushed the door open.

"That's my room," she said. She didn't know why she said anything. Of course he could see it was hers. But suddenly, she felt so awkward, so vulnerable, having him see.

Hagan's eyes darkened as he let his gaze move over Sarah's bed.

It was so obviously hers. So different from the room where he was, from the lacy white bed coverlet to the mound of embroidered pillows that lay atop it. A soft light glimmered through a rose-colored glass lampshade, a sight that looked welcoming. It was a room that was soft and warm and feminine. Just like her.

He recognized the perfume that lingered in the still air. That hint of rain and wild roses, mingled together in a scent so unique and intoxicating that it made him want to breathe it in forever.

So different...so good and clean, after the first fleeting memory of his dirty childhood.

It was a mistake looking into that room.

Hagan turned to look at Sarah, his black gaze meeting hers only a moment before moving down over her breasts and hips and back up again. He didn't say a word, but turned and walked past her toward the kitchen.

When he looked at her that way, Sarah had a problem controlling her pulse and her breathing. Those looks could make her feel hot with confusion and pleasure.

She realized that this was a man who could communicate strictly by senses. Who could install an emotional response that threatened to send her spiraling out of control in a matter of seconds. And that was something she had to be careful about. She countered the feelings by telling herself that Cord would be here soon. That this would be all over and Hagan would be gone.

Yet that thought was anything but comforting.

With a quiet murmur of protest, she made herself move. She also made herself talk. About her own past—rather than Hagan's imminent departure.

"My grandparents lived here from the first day they married more than fifty years ago. My mother was their only child—a divorced mother trying to raise me alone. When she died, they took me in and raised me. I was very young so this really is the only home I remember very well."

Hagan nodded, but his mind seemed elsewhere.

"Are you sure you wouldn't like something to eat? Something to drink?"

"A nice juicy porterhouse would be nice," he said wryly as his gaze moved around the kitchen.

"Actually, I have steak in the freezer," she said, nodding toward the back door that led to the workshop. "But then I suppose you'll be gone before I could manage to thaw it out," she added softly.

His eyes met hers in a look that had absolutely nothing to do with food.

"Yeah, lucky for you," he said. "Where does that door go to?"

Sarah opened the door, revealing a screened and covered breezeway.

"This leads to the workshop. It used to be open, with wild roses trailing over it, but after Grandmother became ill, my grandfather enclosed it so she wouldn't have to go out in the rain to get to her washer and dryer. He wanted to enclose it completely, but she insisted that he screen it so she could still smell the roses. I don't think I ever walk through this breezeway without thinking about how much they loved each other."

Her gaze met Hagan's briefly, then glanced away.

She hoped he didn't ask to see the workshop. She had an easel and paint supplies there. An uncovered painting of a little girl sat unfinished, something she'd started as therapy, and she wasn't ready for anyone to see that yet.

She closed the door and walked to the coffeepot. The delicious scent filled the kitchen. She filled two cups and handed one to Hagan.

"I don't think I've ever been in a house like this," he said.

"My grandparents were simple people," she said. "Gram always said she didn't need much in the way of material things. Just a home with room for a garden and her flowers.''

''I didn't mean that in a critical way,'' he said. ''After the childhood I had, believe me, this looks pretty damn good. I grew up on the mean side of downtown Atlanta, in a neighborhood filled with the kind of people who'd been dealt an unfair hand in life. Poor. Uneducated. And most of them angry. I was a wiseass street kid who'd fight any one of them at the drop of a hat.''

These revelations surprised her. Somehow the picture his words brought didn't fit with the expensive clothes he'd been wearing. Or perhaps that was why he dressed that way... perhaps he had something to prove.

Sarah smiled sweetly.

''It's coming back to you.''

''Just that,'' he said, frowning slightly. ''I don't remember much about school, or work. I can't even remember how I went from the neighborhood where I grew up to being a cop.''

''That transformation from street kid to law enforcement officer does seem rather ironic,'' she said.

''Well, you know what they say... kids in that kind of situation usually end up on one side of the law or the other. In prison or as a cop walking the beat.''

''I'm glad you ended up on the right side,'' she said.

She thought his smile actually held a bit of modesty. And it made her knees weak.

''There's a warmth here in this old house,'' Hagan said. ''An atmosphere that made me feel safe from the first moment I opened my eyes.'' That and you, he wanted to add.

''Yes,'' Sarah said. ''I've always felt that, too.''

''Is that why you came here after your husband died?'' he asked quietly. ''Because you felt safe?''

"Yes, I suppose," she said. She lifted her hand to the scar. "And partly because I wanted to hide away somewhere."

"You must have loved your husband a lot." His words were quiet and oddly tender.

"Yes," she said. "Very much."

"You said it's been a year."

"Yes." Sarah could feel the pain building the way it always did when she wondered why it had to be Joe. The old resentment began eating at her just the way it did when anyone tried to tell her she should be getting over it by now. "But a year's hardly long enough to—"

"Hey," he said. "I'm not judging you. God knows I'm not in a position to judge anyone. Here I'm supposed to be this big tough agent and I can't even remember who tried to kill me. And I know enough about amnesia to know that's probably because I'm too afraid to remember."

She hadn't expected him to say that. She hadn't really expected him to even think of it. But it was true. The wound to his head was not that serious and his amnesia probably had more to do with the trauma he went through that dark rainy night than anything.

"I wish I could help," she whispered. I wish I could love you, take you to my bed, she wanted to add. Make you forget everything and take away that glint of fear and pain I see in those beautiful eyes.

"You have helped," he said. "More than you'll ever know."

They stood for a moment looking into each other's eyes. Hearing only the tick of the clock and the muted sound of birds singing outside.

"Hey," he said, shaking himself. "I'm going to take a shower. Cord will be here and I won't be ready."

"I'll see if I can find some clothes for you," she said, just as blithely.

When she heard the shower running, she placed a pair of jeans and a cotton shirt on Hagan's bed. They were Joe's. Things she'd brought with her out to the farm just to look at and touch. Sometimes, those first dark months, she had taken them to bed with her, clutching them against her as she cried herself to sleep.

They had been precious to her, the only things besides memories, that made her feel close to Joe again. But that closeness had faded over the months and she'd finally laundered the clothes, folded them and put them away. Now she thought she could give the clothes away without feeling any remorse.

She hurried out to the shop to put some of her own clothes into the washer. As soon as she stepped into the building, she reached for a cloth to cover the painting of the little girl. Other similar canvases lay scattered on a table or propped against the wall.

Sarah didn't paint pictures of Joe anymore, or the image of their unborn child. Time had taken away much of the anguish and the sense of loss. The only thing it hadn't banished was her resentment and her anger.

She painted wildflowers now. Masses of exquisite swamp lily, baskets of Queen Anne's lace. Moss-draped live oaks with gray abandoned shacks nestled beneath them.

She'd even done a painting or two of old Tom since he came. Not that he liked it or would sit still for very long. But she thought she'd captured his image very well despite his disapproval.

She smiled as she placed the clothes into the washer and turned it on.

When she went back into the house Hagan was dressed. He was standing near the front door, peering out through the window. For a moment as she saw him dressed in Joe's jeans and shirt, she caught her breath, waiting for the pain to come.

She was somewhat surprised when it didn't. Instead she felt a warm pleasure wash over her. Hagan looked good in the faded jeans. They clung to his hips and emphasized a lean waist and long legs.

But he didn't remind her of her dead husband.

He was Hagan. The man she'd nursed and comforted, a man very different from the husband she had loved. And at the moment, she couldn't find Joe in any sense as she stared at the man at the door. He'd managed to make the clothes his own.

"I see you found the clothes," she said, moving into the hallway behind him.

When he turned toward her, Sarah made a quiet sound. She had always found him handsome, but now, dressed in the soft jeans with the plaid shirt snug across his broad shoulders, she thought he was one of the sexiest men she'd ever seen.

Hagan couldn't quite decipher the look in Sarah's eyes as they wandered over him. Sadness? Pleasure? He wasn't sure.

"I take it these didn't belong to your granddad."

"No," she said. "They were Joe's. I . . . I brought them with me out here to . . . just to have something of him close . . . you know?"

Hagan frowned and ran his hand down his chest over the shirt.

"I hope it doesn't bother you," he said.

"What?" Sarah was still lost in her thoughts and she shook her head to clear them away.

"Seeing someone wear your husband's clothes?"

"Oh . . . no. No, it's all right. It's fine."

If he only knew what she was really thinking, and the guilt she felt for it, he'd be shocked. She certainly was.

Yet despite her guilt, there was a part of her that wanted to be bold, wanted to approach *him*. Seduce *him*. Now. Quickly, before Cord came and the opportunity was lost to her forever.

But another part, that conservative Southern lady part, was afraid. Afraid of rejection. And maybe even afraid of so much more.

She wasn't sure how she would respond now to a man's lovemaking. It had been so long. Yet there was a part of her, locked away deep down inside, that trembled with excitement at the thought.

Sarah sensed that with this man there would be no holding back. No room for caution or halfway measures. He would demand all of her—heart and body and soul. And perhaps that knowledge was what kept her from carrying through with her fantasies—she just wasn't sure she was willing to pay such a price to any man.

"Cord should be here anytime now," Hagan said, as if trying to learn what she was thinking.

"Yes . . . any moment."

Sarah found herself pondering what and who this man was. An officer in one of the South's most respected law enforcement agencies. A man who by nature combined cool, rational thinking with a fierceness that could sometimes be frightening. He lived and breathed danger in his job and because of that she sensed he chose to avoid emotional ties.

He was the kind of man who would take her if she said the word. With raw, untamed sensuality that made Sarah tremble just thinking of it.

But she also sensed that afterward he would kiss her sweetly and tenderly, and then he would simply walk away. Back to the dangerous life that gave him his identity.

"I . . . I think I'd better start breakfast now," she said, turning away.

Hagan watched her. He couldn't explain the sadness that squeezed his heart. And he couldn't even remember if it was something he'd ever felt before.

But he had a strange feeling it wasn't.

Chapter 9

Sarah was just taking biscuits out of the oven when she heard the sound of a car outside. She headed toward the front door, wiping her hands against her apron.

Hagan, who'd been pacing in the hallway, went to the door to look outside and Sarah motioned him into the bedroom.

"Let me make sure it's him," she whispered.

She opened the front door just as Cord Jamison stepped up on the porch. He stopped, lifting his brow with surprise when he saw Sarah. Then he smiled and came toward her.

Sarah thought she'd never felt such instant rapport with anyone in her life. Just looking at the man made her feel safe and warm. It wasn't only his rugged good looks, or the size of him. There was something in his silvery blue eyes, something strong and compelling that she couldn't quite explain. Having him see the scar didn't bother her nearly as much as she'd have thought.

Hagan had that same strength. Yet she felt nervous and uncertain with him.

With Hagan, it's sexual attraction, you fool, she wanted to say. But with Cord there were no underlying emotions to make her feel nervous. She smiled at him.

"May I help you?" she asked. She felt a bit silly doing it. She was positive this was the right man, but with everything that had happened to Hagan she couldn't take a chance.

"I'm Cord Jamison," he said. "You're Sarah?"

"Yes."

"I should have known Hag would manage to find his way into the home of the most beautiful woman in south Georgia."

"Oh my," she said dryly. "Are all the Georgia Bureau boys as charming as you two?"

Cord grinned and reached into his shirt pocket, drawing out a plastic-encased card and holding it in front of her eyes.

Sarah scanned the picture and the other identifying words, then she opened the door and stepped aside.

Once the door was closed, Hagan stepped into the hallway. The two men faced each other, more like enemies than friends.

Cord's eyes studied Hagan carefully and for a moment Sarah was afraid that there might have been a mistake and that the man she'd been protecting wasn't Hagan Cantrell after all.

"Well?" Hagan asked. "Am I the one?"

Cord seemed surprised by Hagan's question and a little troubled by it as well.

"You're him all right," Cord said. His eyes wandered over Hagan's jeans and plaid shirt. "Although I hardly recognized you in such provincial clothes." He glanced down at Hagan's bare feet and grinned broadly. "And I swear I don't think I've ever seen you barefoot before."

Hagan shrugged, but he didn't seem to appreciate Cord's sense of humor.

"You're different, though," Cord said, his look more serious.

For a moment, as the two men stared at each other, Sarah thought Cord meant to embrace Hagan. But Hagan's cool, distant demeanor kept him from it.

"Are you all right?" Cord asked.

"Fine."

"He's remembered a little about his past," Sarah said, her voice becoming clinical and appraising. "But nothing recent."

Cord studied Hagan's closed expression and then he nodded.

"You've remembered Lizzie," he said softly. "I can always tell when you have her on your mind."

Sarah glanced quickly to Hagan. He nodded and brushed his fingers over the corner of his mouth in a self-conscious, troubled gesture.

"Yeah . . . Lizzie."

Cord reached out and put one hand on Hagan's shoulder.

"There are a lot of good things in your life, man," Cord said. "Just because your first memory is a lousy one about your mother and your past, that doesn't mean that's all there is to you. That's what I'm here for . . . to help you remember the good stuff."

Hagan nodded and blew the air out of his lungs, then compressed his lips tightly together. The moment between the two men was so raw and intimate that Sarah felt like an intruder.

"Breakfast is ready," she said. "But if you two would rather talk privately..." She pointed toward the living room, wishing it didn't smell so old and musty.

"That's okay," Hagan said. "We can talk over breakfast, if that's all right with you," he added, looking at Cord.

"Sounds good." Cord smiled at Sarah. "Smells good, too."

Cord did most of the talking as they ate. He seemed intent on helping Hagan remember his past as he regaled them with stories and humorous events from their work together.

But it was obvious Hagan couldn't remember any of it. It seemed to make him uneasy at first and a little awkward. But after awhile, what Sarah sensed more than anything was his growing frustration and anger. Something she could certainly relate to.

Cord saw it, too. He leaned back in his chair, sipping his coffee as he studied Hagan. Cord's gaze turned toward Sarah and she shrugged helplessly.

"I'm not helping, am I?" Cord asked.

"This isn't something you can rush," Sarah said. "It either happens or it doesn't."

"Yeah," Cord said. "It's just that he's so different. Hag has always been the jokester. You know, the one who usually lightens the mood when things get tough."

Hagan was resting his elbows on the table with his mouth pressed against his hands. Now his eyes flickered open and as he straightened, Sarah could see the muscles in his jaws tighten.

"I'm not dead, you two," he snapped. "Or deaf. Or incapable of deciding my own fate. Don't you think it's time we got out of here?" he snapped, addressing Cord now.

Cord's eyes glittered. His teeth pulled at the inside of his lip before he spoke.

"Well, now, there's a problem," he said.

"Yeah, I know," Hagan replied. "And I have it."

"That's not so much a joke as you might think."

"What? Just give it to me straight."

Sarah's gaze moved back and forth between the two men, as if she were watching a hard-fought tennis match.

"I read everything I could find about this case before I left Atlanta. But you know yourself there's nothing like working on the ground. I'm going to need a few days to find out exactly what's going on here."

"I don't think I like the sound of this," Hagan said, shaking his head.

Sarah frowned at the two men. She seemed to be missing something because she didn't understand what Hagan's protest was about at all.

"Look," Cord said. He had become intense, leaning on the table and staring into Hagan's face. "You'd be an easy target right now. At this point you can't distinguish between friend or foe. You could meet the men who tried to kill you face-to-face and you wouldn't even know it. The thing is . . . they'd know you."

"I can go somewhere else," Hagan said. "To a motel or—"

"You'd be safer here."

The room suddenly grew quiet. Hagan turned to look into Sarah eyes and his look was troubled and filled with frustration.

"No way," he said. "I've put her in enough danger as it is. I wouldn't let her notify the sheriff that I was here, for some reason even I can't explain. And when he came out yesterday to check on Sarah, she was put in the position of having to lie because of me."

"Is that right?" Cord asked, glancing oddly at Sarah. "If Hagan had been one of the criminals, that could have put you in a bad situation." He seemed to find her actions amazing.

"I...I don't really trust the sheriff, either," Sarah stammered.

When she glanced at Hagan, he was staring at her with a frowning, incredulous expression.

Quickly she explained about Joe and his investigation. As she spoke, she touched the scar on her face without even realizing it. Hagan and Cord exchanged looks and it was obvious by the look on Hagan's face that this was the first time he'd heard the story. It was also obvious that it bothered him.

Cord leaned back in his chair and whistled quietly.

"He could be the one then," he said almost to himself. "When the undercover assignment went bad, we suspected a leak in the agency, but the investigators swear our house is clean. The local sheriff, or someone in his office, could just be the one who has connections to this Satilla River bunch." He nodded toward Hagan. "You might not have known who you were, pal, but maybe in your subconscious you suspected him all along. Your instincts were right on the mark as usual. This is all the more reason for you to stay where you are until I find out the whole story."

"I said no, dammit," Hagan insisted. There were more reasons for him to go, he wanted to say. Not the least of which was sitting across the table, staring at him with those big, beautiful blue eyes.

"He's right, Hagan," Sarah said. "If you'd stop being so stubborn for a minute, you'd see that."

Hagan glared at her.

"A couple of days," Cord said. "Four at the most."

"I'll be all right," Sarah said. Her words seemed meant for Hagan alone. "Nothing's going to happen."

"Three days," Hagan said to Cord. "If you don't have the goods in three days, I'm out of here regardless."

Cord nodded curtly and stood up. "In that case, I'd better get busy." He smiled at Sarah. "Thanks for breakfast. It was very good. I'll call every few hours to check in. If this mutt here gives you any trouble, you just let me know."

Sarah nodded and said goodbye.

Hagan walked with Cord to the door. Sarah couldn't keep from hearing the conversation even though their words were quiet and low.

"There's one thing I need to know," Hagan said.

"Name it," Cord answered.

"The woman...the agent who was killed...did I know her well? Were we—"

"Hag...why don't we talk about this later," Cord said, his voice low. "When you're feeling better and when I have something solid to tell you."

"Tell me now," Hagan insisted, his deep voice steady.

Sarah noted Cord's frustration...the way he ran his hand through his hair as he stared at Hagan. But then he nodded, seeming to relent.

"There was nothing sexual going on between you if that's what you're asking," Cord said. "Although it wasn't for her lack of trying." There was a wistful humor in Cord's voice as he spoke of the young woman who died. "Cindy was just a kid, cute and sweet—a rookie fresh out of the academy. She had a huge crush on you, though. We used to kid you about that."

"So I didn't...we didn't..."

"Hell, Hagan," Cord muttered. "I'm not sure this is you after all. I can't remember your ever having such an

active conscience before where women were concerned."
He lowered his voice as he glanced toward the kitchen.

"It's just that . . . this amnesia has me buffaloed," Hagan said.

Sarah couldn't move her eyes away from him. She wanted so much to touch him . . . offer him comfort. Even more. She watched as he rubbed his temples, the way he did when he was trying to remember something.

"I thought . . . maybe the reason I couldn't remember was because of her. Because of what happened to her." He shrugged again.

"That still could be the reason, partner." Cord's voice was steady, warmer now and completely devoid of teasing. "You liked her a lot. Kind of looked out for her, like a kid sister. When I heard what happened to her, I was really worried because I knew you'd have died before you'd let anyone hurt her."

Hagan leaned his head back with a loud sigh. His fingers were splayed across his jeans, just beneath the belt loops.

"Yeah? So what happened?" Hagan's voice was flat, with a hint of self accusation.

"We don't know for sure." Cord said. "Unfortunately, you were the only eye witness.

"Listen," Cord continued, clasping Hagan's shoulders. "Don't blame yourself for this. I know you better than anyone and I know for a fact that you'd have done everything humanly possibly to save her. They probably dumped you first and then—"

"No, I don't think so," Hagan said.

"Why?" Cord asked. "Have you remembered—?"

"Flashes here and there," Hagan murmured, his voice quiet. Once he glanced over his shoulder and Sarah pretended to be working. "At first they didn't mean much . . . I

thought they were just nightmares. But now, maybe..."
His voice trailed away and he sighed again. "Look, you'd
better go. We'll talk later. Maybe between the two of us we
can piece this thing together."

"You can count on it," Cord said. "In the meantime,
you might need this." He placed a gun in Hagan's hands.

They shook hands and Cord left. Hagan stood at the
door, peering out past the porch. His hands were jammed
into the pockets of his jeans, shoulders hunched. Sarah
thought he looked like a little boy who'd been left out of
the game.

Even after the sound of the car drifted away, he still
continued to stand there very still.

"Hagan?" Sarah asked, moving quietly into the hallway. "Are you all right?"

"Sure," he said, glancing over his shoulder at her.
"Fine."

He pushed himself away from the door, not quite meeting her eyes as he stepped toward his bedroom.

"I think I'll lie down awhile."

Sarah was left standing in the hall. When he closed the
door to the bedroom, she actually winced, as if he had
physically pushed her away from him.

She busied herself cleaning up the rest of the breakfast
mess and putting the dishes away. She took steaks out of
the freezer, although she wasn't sure Hagan would welcome a steak dinner now. She swept the kitchen floor and
made up her bed.

And all the while what she really wanted to do was peek
into Hagan's room to see what he was doing. Was he
sleeping? Or was he, as she suspected, lying there brooding about what had happened to Cindy and the part he
thought he'd played in her death?

She went to his door several times. Once with the thought of checking his temperature as an excuse.

But each time she turned away. He had not shut her out this way before and she hadn't the courage to intrude on his privacy.

Finally she went out to the workshop, put an old shirt over her clothes and took out a new canvas.

She painted until her head and eyes ached and her back felt stiff from sitting so long. When she went back into the kitchen she could see that Hagan's door was still closed although it was well past noon.

She shook her head and decided to go outside and cut some roses for the table. She had just taken a pair of pruning scissors out of a drawer when she heard a noise from Hagan's room.

She walked quietly down the hall and stood listening outside the door. When she heard him cry out she put the scissors on the hall table and pushed open the door.

He was lying on the bed. She could see his clenched fists against the quilts as he thrashed around.

"Hagan?" she said, moving toward the bed.

She sat down beside him, placing her hands on his shoulders. His teeth were clenched, eyes closed tightly. His muscles beneath her hands were tensed to a rock hardness. He could easily swat her away like an insect, yet still she kept holding on to him.

He felt warm, but she didn't think it was fever that caused him all this anguish.

"No," he said, moving his head back and forth against the pillow. "No!"

Suddenly he sat up, the weight and strength of him almost sending Sarah off the bed. When he saw her, it seemed to take a moment for him to realize who she was and where he was.

"What is it?" she whispered.

Hagan closed his eyes, his breathing fast and hard. He rubbed his hand down his face and then opened his eyes again. Sarah thought she'd never seen such sorrow in anyone's eyes.

"Hagan...?" She reached for him, placing her hands on his chest as she looked into his eyes. Her actions were instinctive, something she didn't even have to think about.

Hagan's mouth opened and his eyes changed. He caught her wrists and pushed her away, the look in his eyes one of warning.

"Get out of here, Sarah," he whispered.

"I want to help you," she said.

"You can't help me," he growled. "No one can help me."

"Just talk to me," she said. "Tell me what happened... what you were dreaming about."

For a moment he seemed to weaken. He released one of her wrists and reached up to touch her face.

"Things you don't ever want to know," he said. There was a sheen of perspiration on his forehead and his eyes were dark and troubled.

"I've worked in a hospital. I've seen every kind of violence you can imagine," she said.

"No," he said with a grimace. "No, darlin', you haven't."

He looked straight into her eyes and gently, but firmly, pushed her away from him.

His look warned that the subject was closed.

"Why didn't you tell me the story behind how your husband died?" he asked. "And your suspicions about the sheriff being involved then?"

"I was planning to," she said.

"When?" he asked. "When he sent some goon out here to make sure you don't talk? When it was too late for me to help you?"

"That's not going to happen," she said.

"God, girl," he snapped. "You've seen firsthand what these people can do." When he touched her scar, his hand was gentle, despite the anger and hardness in his voice. "Are you just completely naive or—?"

"I'm not afraid," she said, despite the pounding of her heart.

"Well, you damn well should be. I know you're not stupid."

"What can they do to me?" she whispered. "Kill me? They did that a year ago. I told you before," she said, tightening her lips together. "I don't care about much anymore...including myself."

He still held her wrists and now he jerked her as if he wanted to shake her.

"You do care, dammit," he said. "I don't know if you really believe that crap, or if you're in a complete state of denial. But you do care, Sarah. Or you wouldn't have taken a stranger in and saved his life and you wouldn't have lied to the sheriff to give me more time."

Sarah couldn't keep her chin from trembling and she couldn't pull away from his tight grip.

"Let me go," she whispered.

He released her so suddenly that she stumbled when she got up from the bed.

"Gladly," he said. "I'm sorry that I have to be here for three more days, and I'm sorry that you have to be involved. You are the one person in the world who doesn't deserve any more grief."

Sarah stood staring at him, her heart aching with her need to touch him. He was so changeable. So unpredictable. In one breath he could make her want him with a passion that threatened to overwhelm her. And in the next, he was hard and angry, pushing her away.

Hagan swung his legs over the side of the bed. He held his side as he looked up at her from beneath his dark brows. "I might not remember everything about myself yet, but I remember enough to know you were right before . . . I'm not the kind of man you need to be mixed up with. So do yourself a favor, darlin', and just stay out of my way these next few days."

His warning, dry and filled with sarcasm, made Sarah flinch.

And yet, there was a part of her that understood and saw through his bitterness.

"You couldn't have saved her, Hagan," she whispered. "Cord said you weren't the kind of man to ever back away when a friend is in danger."

His gaze flickered toward her, hard with warning.

"She doesn't have anything to do with this," he growled. "Or with you."

"Yes, she does," Sarah said. "She has everything to do with it. You're angry and you're feeling guilty. And maybe you're even feeling a little inadequate. I know all about those feelings . . . and what they can do to a person inside."

"Dammit," he muttered. He stood up, as if he might physically remove her from the room, but Sarah stood her ground.

She reached out and touched his face and she could feel him shaking.

"It wasn't your fault, Hagan," she whispered. "No matter how hard you might want to, you can't save the entire world."

Hagan closed his eyes, clenching his teeth. For a moment he swayed toward her and for once he had no response, no hard words to send her running.

"Go away, Sarah. Please. Just get out of here." His voice was soft and filled with a surprising vulnerability.

Without a word of protest, she turned to leave the room, stopping at the door.

"We're having that steak you wanted for dinner," she said, almost shyly. "Maybe we can just pretend for these next few days that there is no G.B.I. and no gunrunners. No Cindy."

Hagan stared at her across the room. He could hear the quiet pleading in her voice, even though he couldn't see what was in her eyes.

"And no Joe..." he replied quietly.

Sarah bit her lip and swallowed hard. Then she nodded. "No Joe," she answered.

Chapter 10

Hagan stood staring at the door long after Sarah was gone.

So...she wanted to pretend there were no problems...no danger. Did she also want to pretend that there was nothing between them? That the air didn't practically sizzle when they were in the same room together?

She sure as hell wasn't making *that* pretense easy.

He already knew that having her around was comforting. That she gave him a peace no one had ever given him before. But there was more to his wanting her than that.

Just looking at her, it was hard to conceal the pleasure he felt. And the need. In fact, Hagan was beginning to think he'd never get enough of looking at her. He found himself wanting to touch that mass of auburn hair. Even now, thinking about it, he felt his fingers curling into a fist, longing to feel the thick beautiful curls. He daydreamed about lifting it and holding its weight against his hand, pushing his face against it and breathing deeply of the clean scent while he held her soft, luscious body against his.

And those eyes. Damn, he thought those blue eyes, so wide and clear, could look right through to a man's soul. Definitely a place he'd never allowed a woman to wander before, he'd be willing to bet.

And her compassion appealed to him just as much as her beauty and sex appeal.

Damn, but he had to get those images out of his mind if he meant to stay here three more days. He had a feeling she was still in love with her husband, no matter how hard she tried to pretend she was over it. He touched his forehead, wondering if it was the fever that was making him feel this way. But he felt cool and perfectly lucid for the first time since he wandered into Sarah's farmhouse.

Hagan sat on the bed. He closed his eyes and tried to push the disturbing images and needs away. He was tired, and weaker than he wanted to admit to Sarah or Cord. One of the most frightening things about being so weak was his inability to protect Sarah if he had to.

And he was beginning to wonder if he'd ever have his memory back.

Cord was like a stranger to him. It made him feel as if he couldn't really trust him. And he didn't like that feeling.

He felt so alone, and oddly that was something he *did* remember. He could remember always being alone. And hating it.

Had he ever gone back to see Lizzie after that day? His mind hadn't yet let him get that far.

Hagan glanced toward the door. He could feel Sarah's presence on the other side pulling at him, beckoning him like some ancient sea siren. He didn't feel alone with her.

He felt warm and contented, as if he could stay here forever, wrapped in the peace that surrounded this old house.

He didn't have to rely on memory to know that was not a good thing for a law enforcement officer to be feeling.

He lay back on the bed and closed his eyes, determined to stay as far away from Sarah as possible for the next three days.

Later, when she knocked on the door and then stepped into the room, he was sleeping. He roused and blinked, noting that she had changed into white slacks and a soft blue sweater. And that she was wearing shoes with straps and tiny little heels. In her hand, she carried a straw bonnet—undoubtedly meant to hide her face from the world.

"I have to go into town," she said, keeping her voice low.

"I don't think that's such a good idea."

"I'll be careful," she said. "I have to go to the grocery store. I haven't been in a couple of weeks and—"

"I'll go with you." Hagan swung his legs over the side of the bed. He groaned as his muscles pulled against the sore ribs.

"You can't do that," she said. She stepped farther into the room, as if to stop him physically. "As much as I'd like some company, I don't think it would be safe."

"I'll wait in the car," he muttered.

"Cord would kill us both if I let you take such a chance." Her smile was sweet as she stepped back to the door, resting her hand on the doorknob. "Besides, I won't be long." A flicker of worry crossed her features and she glanced out toward the hallway.

"I found a box of shells for the shotgun. I put them on the table in the hallway... near the gun."

Hagan reached beneath his pillow and retrieved the gun that Cord had left him.

"Come here."

"Why?" Sarah asked, looking at him suspiciously.

Hagan sighed and stood up, motioning her toward him.

"Come on . . . I'm not going to bite you. Or kiss you," he growled. "Or do anything else you don't want me to," he added sarcastically. He lifted the gun and held it away from him toward the light, smoothing his hand down the barrel as if he didn't want a speck of dust on it anywhere.

"I don't like guns."

"That's only because you don't know anything about them," he said.

"I don't want it," she said, nodding toward the gun. She had walked a few steps toward him, but she was still out of his reach.

"Well, you're taking it whether you want it or not," he muttered. "It's either that or I go with you."

Sarah muttered something beneath her breath, but reluctantly she moved closer. She knew when he had that glint in his eyes that he meant what he said and she had no doubt he would go with her, despite the danger.

"See," he drawled. "No biting or grabbing . . . no kissing. Now," he said, turning his attention back to the gun. "I'm going to show you how to use this. You'll feel better about it if you know how to use it."

"I doubt that," Sarah muttered.

"Just listen," he said. "And pay attention."

Sarah barely saw his hand move, but there was a slight click, and then the gun seemed to spit out a metal object into his hand. He held it between his fingers and waved it in the air.

"This is the clip."

Sarah stared blankly at the piece.

"It holds the bullets," he explained.

"But I thought bullets went into the little cylinder...you know...the one that cowboys twirl just before they shoot the bad guy."

Hagan winced but he couldn't help smiling. He had a feeling she liked nothing better than goading him a little.

"That's cowboy stuff, sugar," he said. "And I ain't no cowboy."

Quickly he went over the details again, explaining every part of the gun and every move.

"You got it?" he asked.

"Yes," she said. "I think so."

He pushed the gun toward her and she took it with her thumb and forefinger, holding it away from her as if it were a poisonous snake.

Hagan stepped forward, cursing quietly beneath his breath, and wrapping his hands around her hands and the gun, as he forced her to hold it tighter.

"You're holding it like a girl," he growled, only half teasing. "Hold it firmly," he said. "As if you mean business. It's all right...see, the safety is still on. Always make sure it is."

Sarah could feel her insides trembling. Not from the gun or her fear of it, but from being so close to this man who confounded her with his masculine appeal.

His touching her, the male scent of him, the feel of his hands on hers, were too much. After a year of self-imposed isolation, after months of telling herself she'd never love again, never be loved again, everything about him simply overwhelmed her.

She could feel the heat and burning need deep down inside her. Building. Moving at breakneck speed.

The quiet moan that escaped her lips took her as much by surprise as it did Hagan.

He looked into blue eyes that were wide with disbelief and questions. She couldn't hide the longing, or the languid heat any more than he could pretend he didn't see it. And feel it.

She looked beautiful in her white slacks and sweater. So feminine. So utterly clean and pure. And the scent of her perfume encircled him like a soft velvet rope, pulling him in, binding him as if it were steel.

Slowly he took the gun from her hands and tossed it onto the bed. His hands moved up her shoulders and neck, holding her face and tangling in her hair.

His mouth was hard and hungry, his kiss raw and brutally honest, just the way Sarah knew it would be. Just the way he was.

He kissed her slowly, thoroughly, his arms holding her hard against his body, his tongue rough and erotic.

Sarah groaned from the exquisite pleasure that flooded through her. She felt as if she were actually melting into him and for a moment, she tried to step back, moving away until her hips were against a tall dresser.

Hagan followed, his hands not releasing her. He positioned himself against her so that she was virtually unable to escape. Then he reached out with his hand behind her head, sighing with pleasure as he grasped that soft, enchanting tumble of hair and pulling her slowly toward him again until their lips were mere inches apart.

"Are you still afraid of me?" he asked. His voice was rough and raw as he spoke.

"You said I'd be safe if I came in," she whispered. "That you wouldn't make me do anything I didn't want to do." Yes, I'm afraid, she wanted to shout. Afraid of the way you make me feel. Afraid if I ever let myself go I'll never be able to stop.

"I lied," he whispered.

She welcomed his mouth as he kissed her hard, his powerful body almost crushing her against the piece of furniture.

His hands moved up from her waist, cupping her breasts as he continued kissing her. When Sarah stepped closer and encircled his waist, she felt his breath against her mouth, heard his slight moan and she pulled away, thinking she had hurt his ribs.

He gave a low muttered protest and pulled her back with an almost desperate force. When he looked into her eyes, he saw such sweetness that for a moment he was stunned.

There was love in those beautiful eyes. Deep, passionate love and tenderness. Surrender. Just waiting for him to take it.

He shook his head, as his senses warred with a conscience he didn't even know he had. He breathed between his teeth as he tried to tell himself all the reasons he should push her away from him.

"I made a bargain," he said, his breath hard and ragged. "For the next few days we were going to pretend that our lives are normal." He wanted her so much he could hardly talk. "I guess I just got carried away. And I'm sorry."

If he'd had any illusions about having a quick, lighthearted affair with this woman, he had absolutely none now. Even without his memory, he knew he'd never had an experience like this with anyone.

That realization shook him more than anything and made him stop what he was about to do. Retreat, his mind warned. Before it's too late.

Sarah looked as if he'd struck her. She had been ready...willing to go with him anywhere he wanted to lead her.

Instead, he stepped back away from her, his hands at his hips as he stood staring into her eyes. He seemed troubled and curiously uncertain.

Sarah could still feel the touch of his mouth on hers. Still feel the tingle where his hands touched her.

"It...it's all right," she forced herself to say. She pulled her gaze away from his, feeling suddenly shy and vulnerable. "I understand. Actually, this is something that happens a lot to...to nurses."

He frowned as he raked his hand over his face.

"Nurses?"

"That's all it is, you know," she said, her voice light and breezy, despite the fact that she couldn't seem to breathe correctly. "A lot of patients confuse their feelings of gratitude for something else."

Hagan knew very well this had nothing to do with her being a nurse. And she knew it, too.

"Oh," he grunted. "Gratitude, huh?"

It's a hell of a lot more than gratitude, he wanted to shout. Much more than that.

But he couldn't say it out loud. He had no right to tell her anything. No right to go any farther when both of them knew he would be out of her life for good in three days. If she hadn't suffered so much this past year, he might not feel such guilt. But he had no right to put her through any more emotional turmoil.

No matter how much he wanted her at this moment, he knew she was the kind of woman who needed a commitment. And he wasn't sure he'd ever be ready to give that to anyone.

Suddenly, inexplicably, a phrase popped into his mind. *Case lover.* He knew it was a phrase that the agents used to identify forbidden love affairs when one of the agents became involved with someone on a case. Usually hot and brief. It sounded awfully familiar to Hagan. And something about it made him feel ashamed.

Sarah James was much too precious to be anyone's case lover. Much too decent and sweet.

He wasn't sure he'd ever done an honorable thing in his life where women were concerned, but this was one time he meant to try.

"Go ahead," he said, backing away. "Go do your shopping. But I still insist you take the gun with you." He walked to the bed, not quite meeting her eyes when he handed the pistol to her. "Keep it under the seat where you can get to it quickly if you need it."

Sarah hardly knew what had hit her. Suddenly her entire body felt heavy and slow, her feet leaden.

Without a word, she took the gun and walked to the door, turning once before leaving.

"There's a TV in the living room," she said, her voice flat. "And books and magazines, too, if—"

"Yeah," he said. "Thanks."

Sarah drove to town, her mind in a daze, her heart and head still reeling from what had just happened. She and Hagan were like moths dancing around a flame. Coming closer and closer with each kiss...each touch. Knowing that any moment the fire might reach out and grab them, and consume them both.

And yet neither of them seemed able to stop what was happening.

At the grocery store, she was glad she had a list. Otherwise she wouldn't be able to remember a thing she came for.

She had pulled her hat down low on the side where her scar was and she was so engrossed in what she was doing that she didn't see her friend Lacy until she heard her voice.

"Sarah?" Lacy touched Sarah's arm, staring at her oddly, as if she couldn't quite believe what she was seeing.

Sarah turned and smiled, telling herself silently that she must not give anything away.

"Well, as I live and breathe," Lacy whispered. Rich brown eyes snapped to life as she stared at Sarah. "I can't believe it's you. Actually out shopping in the middle of the day." Lacy's gaze moved over Sarah and she whistled softly between her lips. "And you look wonderful. Absolutely radiant. Is something going on that I don't know about?"

Sarah blinked and coughed self-consciously.

"Going on?" she asked. "What on earth would be going on? I'm just taking your advice, that's all. You know...getting out and about. How do you like my hat?"

"It's lovely. You look like a breath of summer. I guess I'm just...surprised to see you here."

Sarah pursed her lips and gave Lacy a look of pure innocence that caused both of them to laugh.

"But I'm delighted." Lacy stepped forward and embraced her friend. "Why don't we take in a movie one night, now that you're venturing out in the world?"

"I'd love to," Sarah said. In three days she'd be searching for something to do, and something to keep her mind off the man who would be gone from her house.

"I'll call you," Lacy said.

Sarah paid for her groceries and hurried out of the store. Before anyone else saw her. And before Lacy saw her driving her grandmother's old Buick and wondered why.

Driving home, she was no more than five miles from the farmhouse when she noticed a truck parked off the side of the road beneath a stand of trees. There was a man sitting behind the wheel and as she passed, she thought he seemed to be sleeping.

But something about the man and the truck caused an alarm to ring in her head. And a few moments later when she glanced in the rearview mirror, the truck was pulling out of the isolated road and falling in behind her.

She could feel her heart begin to pound in her throat.

"Keep calm," she whispered. "It's nothing...just a coincidence."

She took her foot off the accelerator and let the lumbering old car slow down, hoping the truck would pass. When it didn't, she reached beneath the seat, pulling the gun out that Hagan had insisted she bring, and laying it on the seat beside her.

"Please, please, please," she whispered, watching the pickup in her mirror. "Just go around."

Finally she was at the farmhouse, and for a moment she didn't know what to do. Should she turn in and risk involving Hagan in a confrontation or should she just keep on driving?

Instinctively she turned the wheel, feeling the crunch of gravel as she turned into the driveway. She did feel braver in familiar territory. And infinitely safer, knowing Hagan was only a few feet away.

She thought her heart would burst right through her chest. But when she looked in the mirror and saw the truck drive on past, she breathed a heavy sigh of relief and put her head down on the steering wheel.

"Dear God," she whispered. "I'm becoming such a scaredy-cat."

She glanced up at the house and saw the slight flicker of a curtain. She knew it was Hagan and for a moment she was afraid he would come out to see what was wrong. She didn't want that...he shouldn't be outside at all. She hurried out of the car and into the house. She'd bring the groceries in later.

He met her at the door and pulled her inside.

"What is it?" he asked, his fingers digging into her arm. "Why were you sitting in the car like that?" He reached up and pulled the hat off her head, tossing it aside on the floor and running his hand over her face as if to make sure she was all right.

"I...it's nothing," she whispered, staring wide-eyed into his questioning eyes. "Imagination." That word, the one Joe always used half jokingly about his suspicions, made her shiver.

"Don't lie to me, darlin'," he said. "Keeping something from me could be dangerous for us both."

Of course, he was right. He was the expert where these matters were concerned. And it was his life that was on the line here.

"Really, it's probably nothing," she said. She looked around and out the window. "There was a truck. I saw it on a side road a few miles back and it pulled out behind me. For a while I thought he was following me, but when I pulled into the driveway, he went on past."

"Was it anyone you know?" he asked. "A truck you've seen in the area, maybe?"

"Lord, there are a lot of trucks in this county," she said, looking troubled. "I didn't recognize it, but that hardly means anything."

"You're shaking," he said, running his hands down her arms.

"I'm fine. Really I am. When the truck wouldn't pass, I put the gun you gave me on the seat. It's amazing how much more secure I felt." She smiled at him, hoping to allay his fears, and hoping to convince herself that everything was fine.

He sighed and closed his eyes. Stepping back, he released her.

"God, woman, you're going to give me a heart attack before this thing is over."

She shrugged her shoulders, grinning girlishly at him. Now that the incident was over, she felt foolish and a little silly.

"I'll bring in the groceries. Why don't you unwrap the steak in the kitchen. It'll give you something to worry about besides me."

He shook his head at her, but when he turned to go, she thought there was a little smile tugging at his lips.

Cord called a few minutes later and Sarah heard Hagan telling him about the truck that had followed her.

"Yeah, I'll keep an eye open," Hagan said into the phone. His gaze moved toward Sarah more than once. "No...I haven't remembered anything else. How about you? Finding anything?"

"What did he say?" she asked when Hagan hung up.

"He's uncovered one man, an ex-member of the gun-runner group, who swears the sheriff used to belong to the Satilla organization."

"You're kidding," Sarah said. She remembered the sheriff's odd words about citizens needing to be armed for their own protection. It should have struck a chord of warning since it was the Satilla group's same credo. But even now, hearing Hagan say the words, she could hardly believe it.

"Problem is, this man and the sheriff are not exactly friends and we can't be sure he isn't just saying this for revenge. He also says he's afraid and Cord is trying to gain his confidence and convince him he'll be protected."

"And will he?"

Hagan shrugged. "I hope so."

She could see that Hagan didn't want to talk about the details and though she was curious, she didn't push him.

Sarah wasn't sure how they managed to make it through supper. It helped, she thought, that the steaks were delicious and her salad fresh and crisp. Both of them were able to keep up the pretense, through the meal at least.

But later, after the dishes were done and when the silence between them turned awkward, Sarah excused herself.

"I think I'll go to bed," she said, not meeting his eyes. "Maybe read awhile. I'm tired and—"

"Yeah," he said. "Me, too."

It was well past midnight when Sarah finally drifted off to sleep, even though she tossed restlessly and kicked at the sheets. She wasn't sure if the noise she heard was a dream and she was so tired that it seemed to take forever to come fully awake.

She sat up in bed, listening. Had it been a dream? Or was it Hagan?

She heard the noise again, loud this time and somewhere definitely near the house.

She bolted from bed, going into the hallway without bothering to grab a robe or turn on a light.

Hagan was already there in the darkness. She thought she saw the pistol silhouetted in his hand and she shivered.

"What is it?" she asked.

She felt his arm go around her waist as he pulled her against him and whispered into her ear.

"Go into the breezeway," he demanded, his voice husky with sleep. "If you hear anything, you get the hell out the back and run as fast as you can. Even if you don't hear anything, if I'm not back in five minutes, you get out. You understand?"

"Hagan...no," she whispered. "You're still not well. Call Cord—he can—"

"Don't argue," he snapped. "Just do as I say. This will be over before Cord can get his clothes on."

That last fatalistic statement made Sarah tremble and it echoed over and over in her mind as she made her way in the darkness to the kitchen. She glanced over her shoulder one last time before opening the door.

The hallway was empty and the front door stood open. Hagan had slipped outside without a sound.

Chapter 11

Sarah stood huddled in the breezeway, peering through the screen and trying to see into the darkness. After a few moments she became more and more aware of an eerie silence surrounding the house. There was only the distant sound of tree frogs and the long, low hoot of an owl somewhere in the swamp.

How benign the normal night sounds were, when someone she cared about could be in terrible danger. Sarah felt as helpless as she ever had in her entire life.

The waiting seemed to take an eternity. She was sure it had been longer than five minutes, but still she couldn't move. Couldn't make herself slip out the back door as Hagan had ordered her to do.

She couldn't leave him here alone, to face whatever had made the noise. How could he think she might?

Slowly she began inching back along the dark breezeway toward the back door. She'd find a knife...anything.

She had barely stepped into the kitchen when she saw the outline of a man's form in the darkness. Her scream was immediate and instinctive.

She felt his hands on her, felt him pulling her around so that her back was against his chest. His hand went over her mouth. But it was gentle and caressing.

"It's just me, darlin'," Hagan drawled, his mouth against her ear. "Relax . . . it's just me."

Sarah went limp. Then she whirled around in his arms as if she might hit him. She heard his intake of breath as she slammed unintentionally against his sore ribs.

"Dear Lord," she muttered. "You're going to scare the life out of me—do you know that? Can't you just come into the room like a normal person and say, hey, it's me . . . Hagan?"

She was shaking with fury and frustration.

She heard his soft grunt of laughter just before he stepped across the kitchen to turn on the light.

"Here's our culprit," Hagan said.

There in the hallway, looking as if he might spring at both of them, was Tom. His fur was ruffled, his eyes wide with fear and distrust as he crouched, ready to pounce.

"You know this cat?" Hagan asked, his voice filled with mischief.

"It's Tom," she murmured. "And he hates being in the house, as you can see."

Hagan's gaze shifted toward Sarah, from where her pink toenails peeked beneath the long white gown, to the lacy bodice that barely covered her lovely breasts.

"So this is old Tom," Hagan said, trying to shake away the image of her. He took a step closer to the cat and it sprang away from him down the hall to the front door. "Not a very original name."

"Well, I never had a cat before. I don't know anything about cat names."

"He's definitely too belligerent for the name Tom. He was fighting like a tiger outside—that's the noise we heard. They knocked over a planter on the front porch." Hagan stared at the frightened cat. "Hey..." he said, looking at her with a questioning smile. "Tiger...now there's a solid, masculine name."

"No," Sarah said. "His name is Tom. Besides, he's so independent he probably wouldn't come to you, no matter what name you call him. He has a mind of his own." She gave a little huff of disbelief. "Do you realize how ridiculous this is? I've just been scared out of my wits, hiding in the breezeway, expecting to have to run for my life. You went outside with a gun. And now, two minutes later, we're talking about the proper name for a silly cat that doesn't like belonging to anyone."

Sarah glanced at Tom who was still huddled by the front door. In the dim lights, his eyes were dull and yellow.

"He wants out."

"How can you be sure? Maybe he likes being warm," Hagan teased. "Maybe he'd like to sleep in your bed tonight...where it's cozy and safe."

Sarah turned to look into Hagan's eyes. For all the teasing quality in his voice, the look in his eyes was dead serious. The glint she saw there almost made her blush.

"I told you," she said. "He's just an alley cat. He doesn't know anything about hearth and home."

"He could learn." Hagan looked at the cat then back at Sarah. "Maybe he's just misunderstood. Maybe he just needs a little TLC. Who knows, he might learn to like domestication."

How had the conversation suddenly changed? And why did Sarah have the distinct idea that they were no longer talking about the cat?

"For a while maybe," Sarah said quietly. "But sooner or later he'd grow tired of the dull peaceful life. Just when I'd begin to get used to him, I might wake up and he'd be gone."

She walked to the door and opened it. Tom ran so quickly that he was only a blur going out into the dark.

"Why would any sane cat do that?" Hagan asked, gazing toward the door. He had moved a step closer to Sarah, his eyes dark and searching. "Why would he go back to the swamp with all its dangers when he had you to come home to?"

"Maybe he likes danger," Sarah whispered. "Maybe it's in his blood and he can't ever change."

"Oh, but I've heard that love can change anything." Hagan stepped closer still, his movement stealthy and graceful—not unlike a great, cautious tiger.

"Cats...cats don't know anything about love," she answered, her breath coming in little gasps. He was so close she could feel the heat of his body against her bare skin. "It's all in the chase and the conquering. It's instinctive. They only want what they can find for one night."

He reached out and placed one finger under the strap of her gown, running it downward and stopping just at the top of the lace.

"Is that so terrible?" he whispered. "One exciting, heart-stopping night?"

Sarah was finding it difficult to breathe, let alone speak.

"People need more than that," she managed to say finally. "They need . . ."

"What?" he urged. "What do people need, Sarah? What do you need?"

"Permanence," she said. She took a deep breath and looked straight into his eyes. "Commitment. And love."

Hagan recognized the look in Sarah's eyes. But that hint of surrender he'd seen there earlier was tempered by something else—by a reluctance that he understood all too well. And he knew she was waiting to hear his answer.

"Then I guess I'm a lot more like old Tom than I thought," he said. "I never knew what love was when I was growing up. Who knows...maybe I still don't. Maybe I'm the kind of man who's incapable of love."

"I don't believe that," she said. She closed her eyes for a moment, breathing in the male scent of him, swaying toward him hypnotically before opening her eyes again.

He looked deep into her troubled blue eyes.

"To be honest, I doubt I would recognize love if it hit me in the face. A woman would have to realize that about me, I guess."

"A woman would be a fool to love someone who felt that way, wouldn't she?" Sarah asked.

"Absolutely crazy," he agreed, his voice soft and hypnotic. Pulling her closer.

She wanted him. God, she had never wanted anything so badly in all her life. Her body was melting, burning with her need to have him touch her, kiss her the way he had before.

Sarah bit her lip and her dark lashes lowered, hiding her eyes from him. He read her emotions all too easily. And she hated for him to see just how weak she was where he was concerned.

She had sworn she wouldn't accept anything less than love and commitment. But now, with her body aching for him, she wasn't so certain about that anymore.

Hagan saw the look in her liquid eyes. There was genuine fear there and it shook him out of his teasing manner.

This wasn't a game he was playing. Sarah deserved more than games. Alley cat games. He'd known that about her all along and he couldn't pretend anything had changed just because his body ached to make love to her.

"And what about you, Sarah? Have you ever felt just a little crazy?" he whispered, his voice soft, his breath brushing against her lips.

"Absolutely... crazy..." Sarah moaned and leaned toward him.

He reached out and wound his fingers into her hair, pulling her head forward.

"Have you ever found yourself wanting something so badly that—?"

"Yes," she whispered.

"Just on the edge of doing something that you know you're going to regret later?"

"Oh, yes." The word came out in one long sigh, one quietly whispered rush. Her hands moved to his chest and she found herself leaning against him. *He* was making her crazy and he knew it. She could feel her insides quivering with emotion. And with something she recognized instantly as pure, undeniable lust.

"God... Hagan," she breathed. "If you don't..."

"What, darlin'?" he whispered, moving close, pulling her body tight against his.

"... shut up and—"

His mouth cut off the rest of her words. The teasing, the tenderness vanished as soon as she felt his lips on hers. They had waited too long, teased too often for that. Now there was only a hot, aching need racing through both of them.

The heat of his body scorched right through the fabric of her nightgown, melding their bodies together and making her gasp with the pure sensuality of it.

After a long year without love, Sarah's body had come alive with tingling pleasure.

Hagan pulled his mouth away from hers and Sarah cried out a soft protest.

Still looking into her eyes, he picked her up in his arms and carried her to her bedroom. She wrapped her arms around his neck as he kicked open the door and carried her inside.

"I should ask if you're sure about this," he said, his voice husky with emotion.

"Don't ask . . ." she groaned.

When she reached up to kiss him, her mouth was hot and sweet. Urgent. And that final kiss broke through any conscience he might have had about what he was doing.

He stood her on her feet and slipped the gown over her head. Slowly his hands and eyes moved over her body as she trembled before him. When he bent his head and trailed kisses down to her breasts, Sarah leaned her head back and closed her eyes. Her fingers grasped his hair to steady herself.

Hagan dropped to one knee, his mouth leaving a fiery trail along her rib cage and down her stomach.

"So beautiful . . ." he murmured against her skin. "So sweet."

"Oh . . . Hagan . . ." she whispered.

Without thinking Sarah dropped to her knees, too. Her fingers raked down his naked chest to the front of his jeans. She felt his quick intake of breath and his eyes opened wide as he stared into her face.

She felt the heat of him, the hardness.

She was still on her knees when he slowly stood up and pushed the jeans off his body. She leaned back, the palms of her hands on the floor behind her, as she let her eyes take in every inch of him. From his muscular legs all the way up his strong, hard body.

When he reached one hand down, she took it, pulling herself up against him and reaching out for his mouth at the same time. When he kissed her eyes and her mouth, she thought she might actually faint from the heat and longing that had built up inside her.

They fell together onto the bed, neither of them willing to wait any longer. She heard his breath quicken as he took her, felt the muscles of his legs hard against hers.

Sarah cried out, her back arching and her hands going up to grasp his shoulders. Her body's reaction was immediate, the convulsions ripping through her again and again.

She could hardly believe it and she made a quiet murmur of disbelief that was almost an apology. She was too needy... too hot.

"No, baby," Hagan said fiercely. "It's good... wonderful." His mouth was hungry and sweet, as if he couldn't get enough of her.

Her response threatened to rob him of all resolve and strength. The pleasure of her body was almost more than he could handle.

There were brief flashes in his mind. Visions of other soft arms reaching for him... other lips parted, different eyes filled with desire. And yet they were nameless visions. Dreams without end or meaning.

Had any woman ever been as sweet? As intoxicating as this one? Was it because he couldn't remember that made this seem so special? So good?

They were right together. Hot and quick and exactly right. As he made love to her, she whispered his name over and over, her little cries of pleasure seeming to come up from her very soul.

Nothing... no one was ever like this before. He knew it in the deepest recesses of his heart, whether his memory followed it or not. Nothing.

"Sweet... Sarah," he whispered, feeling the sensations ripping his body.

Sarah held him close, reveling in the feel of him, delighting in his loss of control. His response made him seem more real and more vulnerable than she ever could have imagined.

"Yes," she whispered. "Oh... yes."

Afterward Hagan lay holding her, trying to breathe, trying to reconcile what had just happened with who and what he was. When he rolled away, he put his arm beneath her and looked into her face.

She was smiling, but there were tears sparkling in her dark eyelashes.

Hagan frowned and reached out to brush them away.

"What?" he whispered. "Did I hurt you? Was I—?"

"No," she said, pulling his hand away and kissing his fingers. "No, you didn't hurt me. You were wonderful... unbelievable."

"Then what is it?" He moved down beside her, holding her close as his hand trailed down her arm.

Sarah shrugged her shoulder and hid her face partially against his chest. The reaction was shy and sweet and it caused Hagan to stare at her oddly.

"This might seem like an odd thing to say, but I'm just so thankful," she whispered. "I feel alive. For the first time in over a year, I feel alive again."

Hagan reached down and touched his lips softly to hers. When she turned on her back he pulled the sheet over them, then turned off the light and closed his eyes. He was spent . . . as weak as a kitten.

But he felt alive, too. And he didn't have to remember anything to know that sex had never been like this for him before. As he fell asleep, he realized he didn't want to remember other times . . . other women. Not now . . . maybe not ever. He wanted to pretend that Sarah was his first lover. Because she was the kind of woman every man dreamed of for that first sexual experience—someone good and sweet and completely giving. Yet a woman who was as sexy and sensuous as she was virtuous.

The sound of thunder woke both of them a couple of hours later. Sarah stirred in his arms, then sighed and snuggled against him. Hagan smiled into the darkness as he listened to the wind in the trees and heard the distant thunder moving nearer.

He thought she had gone back to sleep, but when he kissed her cheek, she turned slightly, letting her lips meet his.

When they made love this time, it was slower and more tender. The urgency was still as great, but the fire that had passed between them for days now was banked and quiet. Waiting to be fueled.

Outside the rain came, beating against the house, blowing against the windows and encasing them in a warm, cozy cocoon.

Later when Sarah lay in his arms, she was fully awake. She didn't want to sleep. She didn't want to waste one minute of their time together.

"I can't believe this has happened," she said quietly, pressing her lips against his chest.

"I didn't intend for it to," he said.

"I know. Neither did I," she murmured.

"It's that damn cat's fault," he teased.

Sarah sighed. "Oh, Lord...I was so afraid when we heard the noise. Afraid something would happen to you and I'd never—"

"Shh. Nothing happened. We're safe now. I should probably thank old Tom in the morning."

Hagan pulled away and looked down into her face. A small night-light burned in the room and he could barely make out her features.

"We're quite a pair, aren't we?" he teased. "Dancing around this for days...a man who can't remember his past and—"

"And a woman who would like to forget hers."

"You wouldn't really," he said, tracing a finger down her cheek.

"Why wouldn't I?" she asked.

There had been times this past year when Sarah thought she couldn't cry anymore. And times when she thought she'd never be able to stop crying. Yet despite her pain, she was still here, still trying to make it through each day.

"You don't seem like the kind of person to run away from anything," he said.

"I've been managing to run for a year now," she said, her voice quiet and reflective. She hadn't told him about the baby. Somehow she couldn't find the words. And now that she felt closer to him, she was afraid his kindness and sympathy when he knew, would be more than she could handle.

He felt the delicate bones in her shoulders as she moved restlessly, then sat up in bed. He couldn't resist reaching to touch her breasts, or letting his hand trail down to her stomach.

Sarah felt the catch in her chest. Felt the warmth from his hand spreading through her entire body.

She was falling in love with him. With this mysterious loner who had admitted that he couldn't settle down anywhere. Did she really think that a sophisticated man like Hagan Cantrell, with his five-hundred-dollar suits and Italian shoes could ever be happy living on a farm, with a woman like her?

Had she made the biggest mistake of her life tonight?

She wanted him. Physically, she told herself. But she also found herself longing to be close to him emotionally and she thought that was what she had missed most this past year. That feeling of bonding between a man and woman when they become intimate. And even more when they became friends.

And now what? Would he still leave in three days and never feel the need to look back? Would she be able to let him go without drowning again in that dark hole of despair?

Sarah needed something that would last. While Hagan wanted . . . what?

"Come here," he said, pulling her down beside him. "Talk to me," he whispered against her hair. "Tell me what happened before you came here to forget. Tell me everything. I want to hear."

"Hagan . . ." she protested. It was almost as if he had read her mind. Did he really want to know? Or was he only being kind?

"Tell me," he said, holding her tightly against him.

"I . . . I don't know where to start."

"Start at the beginning. When you were a little girl. When you met Joe. Did you have a big church wedding? Was everyone in town there?"

Sarah laughed quietly, the memories coming to her at his urging.

"Practically," she said. Haltingly, at first, she began to talk about her childhood. About the good times.

Hagan closed his eyes, wanting to feel those good images. Wanting to believe that there were memories and happy lives somewhere still worth holding on to. Hoping that something Sarah said would trigger a similar response in him. And yet knowing in his heart that there were no good memories in his childhood, no matter how hard he wished for them.

He was acutely aware of the softness of her body in his arms, the way her breasts felt against him. That enticing rose scent still lingered in his nostrils and he could almost taste her lips.

He grew so quiet that Sarah stopped, glancing at his closed eyes and placing her hand on his chest.

"Are you asleep?" she murmured.

"Don't stop," he said, still not opening his eyes. "I'm not asleep."

Sarah smiled and snuggled against him again. It didn't seem odd telling him about Joe. Talking about him and their life made her feel good. For the first time in months, she actually could remember their life together with a smile and with sweet nostalgia.

When Sarah woke up the next morning, still wrapped in Hagan's arms, she thought both of them must have fallen asleep in the middle of her remembrances. She couldn't recall where she'd stopped and she didn't remember going to sleep.

She smiled and reached out to touch his chin, letting her fingers move upward to his mouth. He had just opened his eyes when they heard the knock at the front door.

"Oh, my Lord," she whispered.

Before she had time to protest, Hagan was out of bed, hopping about on one foot as he tried to push his leg into the crumpled jeans that had been discarded on the floor.

"Stay here," he said, his voice still husky with sleep.

She pulled the sheet up over her breasts, watching him as he buttoned the jeans, then grabbed his gun from a dresser and stuck it in the waistband at the small of his back.

"Don't open the door," she said. "Until you—"

Hagan grinned wryly at her and she clamped her teeth together, feeling foolish and helpless. Of course he wouldn't just open the door to anyone. He was a trained agent, for heaven's sake.

Yet seconds later that was exactly what he did. She couldn't believe it when she heard the unmistakable sound of the front door opening.

She stiffened in bed, holding the sheets tightly against her naked body as her eyes stared widely toward the open doorway.

Hagan appeared in the doorway, gazing at her almost apologetically.

"It's Cord," he said.

"Oh, no," she whispered, closing her eyes. "Oh, no."

"It's all right," he said. "Give me a minute. I'll put the coffee on while you get dressed."

"But…he…he knows," she whispered. Her eyes moved over Hagan's bare chest and wrinkled jeans. He looked rumpled and his eyes were still sleep-filled.

"Oh, yeah," Hagan answered dryly. "It didn't take him long to figure it out."

Chapter 12

"What in God's name do you think you're doing?" Cord asked. He stood in the kitchen, watching Hagan spoon coffee into the coffeemaker. "I always knew you didn't have much sense about women, but this isn't just any woman."

Hagan slammed the coffee down on the counter and turned around, his eyes blazing.

"You don't have to tell me that," he said. "I know what kind of woman Sarah is. I certainly know more about her than you do."

"Yeah, that's obvious."

"Just stay out of it."

"Oh, stay out of it?" Cord sneered. "Do you have any idea how she got that scar?"

"Of course I know." Hagan said defensively. "Do you think I wouldn't ask ... or that I wouldn't care? Not that it has anything to do with—"

"I've been checking around. And I heard enough to know that the car wreck that gave her the scar also took her husband's life. And I know that his death shattered her so badly that she's given up a nursing career to hide away out here in the sticks."

"Yeah, I know that."

"Then where in hell are your brains?" Cord snapped. His gaze moved over Hagan's bare chest and down to the front of his jeans. "Oh, don't tell me. I guess that's one thing amnesia hasn't changed."

"You know, I'm getting a little sick of your condescending attitude, Jamison," Hagan said.

"Well, then we're even 'cause I'm getting a little sick of your attitude toward women."

"That sounds like Georgia talking to me." Hagan sneered.

"Oh, so you don't remember me but you remember my wife?"

"Yeah, I remember Georgia. What man wouldn't remember Georgia? And I've remembered enough about you, pal, to know you weren't exactly saintly, either, where women were concerned, before Georgia came back into your life."

Sarah opened the door of her bedroom, peeking toward the men in the kitchen. Cord and Hagan became silent when she hurried across the hall to the bathroom without glancing at either of them.

"Do you think she heard us?" Cord asked.

"I hope not," Hagan said, running his fingers through his disheveled hair. "She's embarrassed enough by having you find us in this...situation. I don't want her hurt, Cord."

"No?" Cord's dark brows lifted. "Well, maybe you should have thought of that before you hopped into bed with her."

"Dammit . . ." Hagan took a step toward Cord, his fists clenched as he took a deep breath of air.

The bathroom door opened and Sarah peeked out.

"Will you two please stop it?" she said. "You sound like two little boys arguing over a game of marbles. I'm a grown woman, perfectly capable of making my own decisions and my own mistakes, thank you," she said, scowling directly at Cord.

She slammed the door and left the two men staring blankly at it.

"Well, I guess that settles that," Hagan murmured with a hint of self-satisfaction..

"Hell, no, it doesn't settle anything," Cord said, keeping his voice lower this time. "This is only going to get more and more complicated, Hagan. It isn't going to get any better."

"Don't lecture me. I know what I'm doing."

"Do you?"

Hagan sighed heavily as he leaned back against the kitchen counter.

"Look, this isn't something we planned. It's not like I've been plotting night and day to get her into bed." He glanced across at Cord. "It just happened."

"Yeah, I've heard that before."

Hagan stared hard at Cord, forcing him to meet his gaze. Finally Cord shook his head as a slight smile tugged at the corner of his mouth.

"This is different," Hagan said quietly.

"How would you know?" Cord scoffed. "You can't even remember."

"I just know it—all right?" he snapped. "Besides, I'm remembering a little more every day. Faces at first, then names. I remember Tracy."

"Oh . . . Tracy?" Cord's brows were lifted and he nodded. "Now there is a woman worth remembering, as I recall. And the only woman you ever had a halfway normal relationship with, if I'm not mistaken. What ever happened to her, anyway?"

"That I'm afraid I *don't* remember," Hagan said. Suddenly he laughed and crossed his arms over his chest. "Did you and I always spat like this?"

Cord chuckled, too. "Yeah, pretty much. Mostly when we first met and found out we'd be working together. I was a country boy straight out of the marines and you were a wiseass street kid from Atlanta. We didn't exactly have a lot in common."

"Probably made a pretty good mix, though."

"Yeah, I guess it did," Cord agreed. "Must have we're still kickin' after ten years. Until you went and got yourself shot."

Hagan's eyes grew more serious.

"You still don't remember?" Cord asked.

"No . . . not that part. Not much about the agency, either . . . or you, for that matter. Oddly I remember Georgia and your wedding."

"That's because it's nonthreatening," Cord said.

Hagan's brows lifted in a questioning look.

"I spoke to Dr. Rennig . . . our staff psychologist . . ."

"Oh," Hagan said, nodding. "And what else did Dr. Rennig have to say about amnesia?" Hagan glanced toward the bathroom door. "When I begin to remember, will I still know about this . . . about being here?"

"Sure you will," Cord said. He watched the expression on Hagan's face, noting with surprise his unusual reflection of concern.

Hagan took a long, deep breath of air and turned to pour a cup of coffee.

"That's good," he murmured. "Because if getting my memory back means I would forget this, then—"

Cord studied his partner's profile as he reached to pour himself a cup of coffee, too.

"Forget Sarah, you mean?" he said.

"I don't want to forget being here, or being with her," Hagan said. "Because memories are probably all I'll be able to take away from this place."

Sarah opened the bathroom door. She had noticed earlier that the sound of Cord's and Hagan's voices had quietened and she hadn't been able to make out what they were saying. But with the door open she heard Hagan's last sentence and for a moment she wanted to cry.

Nothing had changed for him. He was still going away and last night hadn't meant the same to him as it had to her.

She gritted her teeth and took a deep, shuddering breath.

She had known all along how it was with him. And somewhere in the back of her mind she'd reminded herself of it last night. Just before they made love. Just before she realized that she didn't want to play it safe any longer.

Hagan wasn't the one who'd changed. She was.

So now she'd just have to live with it.

"Good morning," she said, stepping out of the bathroom.

She had showered and was dressed in faded jean shorts and a loose-fitting white cotton shirt that nevertheless emphasized her breasts.

She smiled at Cord as she walked toward them, but she was finding it difficult to meet Hagan's eyes.

She would have liked them to be alone this morning. To have a few moments to adjust to this fragile new relationship between them.

Maybe even to fall back into bed and make love again.

Hagan was watching her, noting the slight flush on her cheeks and the fresh-scrubbed look of her skin. Not to mention the way her cutoff shorts clung to her hips and emphasized the golden color of her thighs.

When she met his eyes, he felt as if he'd been punched. Her eyes this morning reflected everything that had happened between them during the long, delicious night. The blue depths sparkled with warmth and a look meant only for him.

Hagan frowned. He'd seen that look before. Seen blue eyes like that before that gazed at him with desire and longing. A woman with blond hair and blue eyes.

Was it Cindy he remembered? The sweet, naive young agent who'd had a crush on him? He couldn't quite grasp a clear vision of her—it seemed to float away almost as quickly as it came.

Sarah, on the other hand, he couldn't seem to forget.

He turned and poured her a cup of coffee, placing it on the table as she pulled out a chair to sit down.

"I'm sorry about this morning," Cord said, shrugging his broad shoulders.

Sarah lifted her hand, brushing away his apology with a weak smile.

"It's all right." Her gaze flickered up toward Hagan. "Have you learned anything new?"

"New?" Cord seemed as distracted by Sarah as Hagan was. He looked at his partner and they both grinned, then sat at the table.

"Oh, new," Cord muttered. "As a matter of fact, I wanted you to help me with that," he said.

"Me?" she asked, wide-eyed.

"I want you to tell me everything you remember about the guy who followed you home yesterday. Even the smallest detail."

Hagan watched Sarah. He liked the way she didn't hesitate. The way she pushed her heavy hair back from her face. She seemed to have forgotten the scar and he was glad she felt secure enough with him and Cord to do that.

He had to look away from her to keep from remembering the way her hair felt against his naked skin. This was not the time, he told himself, to be thinking of last night and all the evocative sensations those thoughts brought.

"It was an older truck," she was saying. "A Ford, I think. Red, but it was faded. You know, as if it sat out in the sun a lot."

"How old?"

Sarah shrugged. "Gosh, I don't know. Not as old as Grandpa's—I think he bought his in the seventies. It was the first new truck he'd ever bought," she added softly.

"Eighties then?" Cord asked, taking notes in a small pad he'd pulled from his pocket.

"Yes, I think so. Probably early eighties."

"Describe the man," Cord said, pencil poised.

"Oh, heavens," Sarah said. "I wish I could remember. I was just so scared . . ."

Her eyes darted toward Hagan. His smile was sweet and encouraging.

Suddenly Sarah's expression changed and she turned to look down the hall toward the front door.

"I heard something," she said. "It sounded like a car door."

They all heard the footsteps on the porch and then a heavy knock at the door.

Sarah turned to them, her eyes wide with concern.

"It's all right," Hagan said. He stood up and placed his coffee cup in the sink, then moved silently to the back door. He didn't open it, but stood in the shadows as he motioned Sarah and Cord to go to the door.

Sarah's heart skittered wildly as she walked toward the front door. Cord's presence just behind her gave her less confidence than she would have thought. She had a sudden vision of someone barging through the front door and shooting both of them.

She shook the thoughts away, glancing at Cord once before reaching for the door.

"I'm a friend, visiting from Valdosta," he said, his voice a whisper. "In case anyone asks."

Sarah nodded and opened the door.

Her heart was pounding and her mouth felt dry as she faced the man standing on the porch. He was a big man, as tall as Cord and much heavier. His faced was shadowed by the brim of a ball cap and around his fatigue-clad middle was a belt with a wide leather scabbard. The kind that held a hunting knife.

"Yes," Sarah asked. "May I help you?"

The man took off his hat and made a small, but polite nod to her. His eyes skimmed over Cord, then back to Sarah.

"*Miz* James?"

"Yes, I'm Sarah James," she said.

"How do, ma'am," he said. "Sheriff Metcalf said you had an old truck . . . wasn't runnin' good?"

Sarah wasn't sure what she'd expected. But it wasn't this. For a moment she couldn't speak.

"I . . . well, yes I did have, but . . ."

"Said it was a Dodge."

"Yes," she answered.

"Well, see, I been lookin' for an old Dodge to fix up. Me and the sheriff was havin' a conversation about trucks...kind of a hobby of mine. He just mentioned yours, said you'd been havin' some trouble with it and thought you might be interested in sellin'."

"No," she said. "I really don't want to sell it—it belonged to my granddad."

"I knowed your granddad," he said, his voice kind and sympathetic. "He was a fine old gentleman."

"Thank you."

Sarah relaxed a bit. Was she was becoming so paranoid that even this polite man made her suspicious?

He continued standing on the porch and Cord stepped forward.

"She's not interested in selling," he said.

"Yeah, I know," the man replied. "But I'd like to look at it, anyway. That is if you don't mind. I just kind of like lookin' at old trucks."

Had the man's expression changed? Was his glance at Cord filled with suspicion, or was it just Sarah's overactive imagination?

"Actually, the truck isn't here right now."

"Oh."

The man hesitated. He glanced around the porch and out toward the garage and for a moment Sarah wasn't sure what he intended.

"Well, thanks anyway," he said, after what seemed an eternity. "Mornin' to ya."

"Good morning," Sarah said, watching him go.

She felt Cord brush against her as he walked out onto the porch. The man had left his truck parked near the road and Sarah couldn't see it from the doorway. She assumed Cord was checking it out.

"Say," Cord called to the man. "We didn't get your name. Just in case she decides to sell the truck later."

The man didn't hesitate, but smiled and nodded. His actions made Sarah certain that his visit was legitimate.

"Emmitt Walsh," he said. "Live just the other side of Wayland, in the Bell Oak community. Name's in the book."

Sarah watched the man disappear around the corner of the house. Then she was aware of Hagan standing behind her in the hallway, his hand at her waist, his chin touching her hair.

She leaned back against him just for a moment and felt his hands tighten on her waist. She thought she even felt a soft kiss against her hair.

Cord came back inside and Sarah locked the door.

"Did you see him?" Cord asked Hagan. "Did his voice ring any bells?"

"I saw him," Hagan said. "But no . . . no bells."

Sarah thought he looked pale as he leaned his shoulder against the wall, glancing first at Cord, then at Sarah.

"I still can't remember a damn thing about that night." Hagan's smile, as he pushed away from the wall, was crooked and a bit wry. "But I do remember the camouflage getup from being here on surveillance. They all do seem to use the same designer, don't they? Rambo, if I'm not mistaken. Camouflage fatigues and a great big old knife."

"Yeah," Cord said. He seemed thoughtful and not quite as amused.

"I don't think this man had anything to do with it," Sarah said. "He just seems like a nice, honest man who's interested in buying a truck. A lot of people around here dress in fatigues. And a lot of men carry hunting knives. This isn't exactly metropolitan Atlanta,'' Sarah added, her smile conciliatory.

"It does seem like a big coincidence that the sheriff would send him out here to look at your truck," Hagan said.

"Did you notice he parked out near the main road?" Cord said. "Maybe where you couldn't get a good look at his truck?"

Sarah frowned.

"But why would he—?"

"It was a 1981 Ford pickup," Cord said. "Red and washed-out...as if it had been sitting in the sun for years."

Sarah's mouth opened and she turned to stare into Hagan's eyes.

"But...but he wasn't the man following me...I'm sure of it. The man was younger...with darker skin."

"I'll tell you what we're going to do," Cord said, rubbing his chin thoughtfully. "I'm going to check out this license plate. I'm also going to check out Mr. Emmitt Walsh...see what kind of reputation he has around Wayland. May I use your phone?"

"Yes...sure," she said, pointing to the phone in the hall.

Sarah and Hagan listened, not touching or looking at each other, but standing awkwardly as if neither of them knew what to say or do.

"Hey, Maggie, it's Cord," he said into the phone. "Run this tag for me, will you? Yeah, I'll wait."

A moment later, he wrote something in his notebook and when he turned to Hagan, there was a look of satisfaction in his eyes.

"The owner of the truck is named Dan Brennan," he muttered with an arch of his brow. He lifted his finger and began to dial another number. "This is long distance," he said to Sarah. "I'll reimburse you. I just want to check in with my wife."

"No problem," she said.

Hagan reached for her hand, pulling her with him toward the kitchen.

"Come on, let's have a cup of coffee. I have a feeling this conversation is going to be private."

In the kitchen they could hear Cord's words, even though his back was to them and his voice was lowered.

"Hey, baby, it's me."

"Yeah, I miss you, too…like crazy." There was a pause. "He's fine." Cord turned and grinned at Hagan. "As a matter of fact he's standing right here. Georgia says hi," Cord said.

"Tell her I still say she married the wrong man," Hagan said, grinning.

Hagan and Sarah took their coffee and sat at the table, ignoring the rest of Cord's conversation. He reached to take her hand.

"This morning didn't turn out exactly the way I intended," he said.

"I know," she whispered, looking into his eyes. "But maybe it was best. I didn't know what I was going to say to you."

Hagan turned his head and frowned.

"You're not sorry, are you? Because if you are—"

"No," she whispered. She reached out to touch his unshaven face, letting her fingers trace a line along his stubbled jawbone. "I'm not sorry. Not for one minute."

"Your fingers are shaking," he said. "Are you all right? Did the man at the door frighten you that much?"

She smiled at him.

"No, maybe I'm getting used to this craziness. I'm not shaking because I'm afraid," she said softly.

"Oh," he said, with a teasing arch of his brow. "That's okay then." He kissed her, then his look grew more serious. "Look, this is all going to be over soon," he whispered. "I promise."

Hagan was surprised at just how protective he felt toward Sarah. He knew Cord was right when he tore into him this morning. It was hardly professional to go to bed with someone involved in a case. If the agency preached anything, it was not to get involved or get too close, no matter what the circumstances were.

Funny, but his body didn't seem to be paying attention.

He might not be able to remember everything yet, but he still knew himself better than anyone. And he knew that deep down inside he was not one to become involved. For all his outward pretense at charm and camaraderie with the other agents, he was a cautious man, and except for Cord, happiest when he was alone. Distrustful, with barriers and guards to keep people at arm's length.

A man who, on one hand, smiled and motioned people in. But on the other hand, a man who always put on the brakes. Who decided when a relationship would begin and when it would end.

And he wasn't sure how this woman had slipped past those barriers so swiftly and so easily.

Was it because he'd been practically dead when he came here? Had it been gratitude at first? Comfort?

Feeling the way his body responded even now to the touch of her hand, he knew it was more than that.

This had not been the normal cajoling, teasing game of getting a woman into bed. And although the sex had certainly been just as hot and exciting, something was very different.

This time he wasn't playing games.

Somehow he had let himself become vulnerable. And he couldn't afford to let that happen again.

Cord hung up the phone and walked into the kitchen.

"Sarah, I need your help."

"Of course... anything."

"Now wait a minute," Hagan said, bristling. "I thought I made it clear that she's not to be involved anymore."

Cord ignored him and continued talking to Sarah.

"I really need you to do this. We're going to find this Dan Brennan and you're going to tell me if he was the man driving the faded red truck that followed you. If he was and Emmitt Walsh was driving it today, then I have to believe they're on to us. We need to act quickly before they meet with the rest of the group and put two and two together."

"I'm going with you," Hagan said.

"No." The word was spoken by Cord and Sarah at the same time.

"Yes, dammit," Hagan said. "I can't just sit here like—"

"It's too dangerous," Cord said. "You're the one they're looking for. Even if they do see Sarah in town they won't be sure why she's there. But with you coming out in the open, you'd just be asking for it."

"He's right, Hagan," Sarah said. "Please... listen to him."

Hagan gritted his teeth and closed his eyes. Sarah wanted nothing more than to go to him. She didn't care what Cord saw or what he thought. All she could think about was Hagan and what he must be feeling.

But something prevented her from doing that. Maybe it was because they hadn't really had time to talk about what was happening between them. Maybe it was because in her heart she was still afraid that it might have only been a one-night stand as far as he was concerned. Just a passing fling until this case was settled and he moved on to another one.

"I'll be fine," she said. "Cord won't let anything happen."

Hagan opened his eyes and stared up at his partner.

"He'd damn well better not."

"You're the one who needs to be careful," Cord said. "You'll be alone here for a couple of hours at least. When we get back, we'll decide if we have to move out of here or not. In the meantime, you watch it, you hear?"

Hagan sighed, but it was obvious he still didn't like it.

"I hear you."

Cord was discreet enough to go outside for a moment, leaving Sarah and Hagan alone.

Hagan stood up and reached for her, pulling her up and into his arms with a heavy sigh.

"I don't like this, darlin'," he said. "I don't like it a damn bit."

"I know. I don't, either. But I'll be all right."

His kiss was sweet and tender and when he looked into her eyes, Sarah felt her heart skip a beat.

"I'll see you in a couple of hours," she whispered as she reluctantly pulled away.

"I'll be waiting."

Chapter 13

It was late afternoon when Cord and Sarah drove back toward the farmhouse.

"I'm sorry it took longer than I thought," Cord said. "Unfortunately, Dan Brennan doesn't hold down a steady job, so he was harder to find than I expected."

"I'm just a little worried about Hagan, that's all," she said, gazing hard into the distance, waiting to see the little house come into view.

"You don't have to worry about Hagan," Cord said, glancing at her. "He can take care of himself. Now that you've identified Dan Brennan as the man who followed you, we need to get both you and Hagan out of here as soon as possible."

Sarah bit her lip.

"I can't believe Emmitt Walsh is involved in this. He seemed like such a nice man."

Cord shrugged. "He could be a nice man. Some people

who join these groups lead pretty normal lives. They're just easily manipulated and a little misguided, that's all."

"Dangerously misguided," Sarah said.

"In this case, you're right," he said.

When they pulled into the driveway, Sarah had her hand on the door handle, waiting to spring from the sedan.

"See," Cord said. "Everything is normal. Although I'd be willing to bet Hagan is wound up as tight as an eight-day clock by now."

As soon as Sarah stepped onto the front porch, an odd feeling swept over her. It seemed quieter than usual. The birds weren't even singing in the trees around the house.

She glanced toward Tom's box but he wasn't there. She cocked her head curiously as she noticed the odd angle of the wooden box and how the old pillow that usually lay inside was partially out on the floor.

She reached for the door, then felt Cord's hand grab hers. The door was open about an inch and the wood around the lock was splintered. Then she saw it—the outline of a black shoe-print against the dusty white woodwork. Sarah's heart almost stopped when she saw the look in Cord's eyes and saw him reach for the gun he carried beneath his jacket. She gave a soft cry of protest, unable to believe what was happening. It was almost like a slow-motion dream . . . like the accident that took her husband's life.

Cord had to hold her back out of the way, as he nudged open the front door with his foot, then stood aside, gun held upward.

"Hagan?" he called.

Sarah stood on the porch with her back against the house.

"Please," she whispered to herself. "Please let him be all right."

"Stay here," Cord said as he stepped inside the house and flattened himself against a wall in the hallway.

"Hag?" he yelled, louder this time. "You here?"

Sarah was trembling. She clasped her hands together against her mouth to keep from crying out. If something happened to Hagan while they were gone, she'd never be able to forgive herself. And she knew from the desperation in Cord's voice that he felt the same way.

"Keep your eyes open out there, Sarah," she heard Cord say. "Let me check this out."

It seemed like an eternity before he came back

"He's not here," he said, his eyes narrowing as they scanned the trees around the house.

Sarah's sigh of relief was also tinged with fear. She stepped inside the hallway and gasped. What she saw made her knees tremble so badly that she had to hold on to Cord to keep from falling.

"Oh, my God," she whispered.

Slowly her gaze moved around the house. There didn't seem to be one spot that hadn't been disturbed, or one piece of furniture that wasn't overturned.

She grasped Cord's shirtsleeve.

"They've found him," she said. "They figured out he was here and they've taken him. Oh, Cord," she whispered, her eyes stricken. "They'll kill him this time. They won't take a chance on him getting away again."

"I don't think so," he said. "If they'd found him, why would they have torn up the house this way? Besides, I know Hagan better than I know anyone. He has a sixth sense about danger and unless I miss my guess he probably saw this coming. Looking at the window in the shop out back, I think he went out that way... maybe into the woods."

"Show me," she said, moving toward the kitchen and the back door.

Cord grabbed her arm.

"Sarah, wait. We have to get out of here. They could be watching the house even now."

"I'm not leaving until you show me what you mean," she said, pulling away from him. "Those are not just woods out there, Cord, it's swampland. Do you know how much danger he could be in if he's lost in the swamp?" She shivered. "He won't be much better off there. It will only take longer." Her voice trembled and her eyes were filled with terror.

It was that pleading look in her eyes that made Cord follow.

The screen door from the breezeway to the yard was still latched from the inside. But the workshop had been ransacked. Sarah's easel was shattered and her canvases lay strewn around on the floor.

Sarah knelt and turned over one of the canvases, one of the many idealized portraits she'd painted of herself with Joe and their little girl. An imagined portrait of a child she never knew. The hope of a family that would never be.

She gritted her teeth and stood up, angry now. The freezer door stood open.

Sarah went to close it as Cord pointed to a back window. The window was closed, but upon closer inspection she could see what he meant. The screen had been cut carefully, then pushed back into place to make it appear whole.

"See this little mark on the windowsill?" he asked.

"It looks like an *H*," Sarah said.

"Hag and I used to have a code," Cord said. "Back when we were rookies and both working undercover, if we were ever separated, we'd always try to leave our initials, somewhere, somehow, to show the other which way we went."

"But he doesn't remember any of that," she said.

"Maybe he does now. It can happen that way, can't it? When everything comes back at once?"

"Well...yes. But the wood on the window is so old and scratched..." Sarah felt her heart leap, even though she was telling herself to be cautious. "How can you tell if—"

"I guess it's more a hunch than anything," Cord said.

Sarah heard a sound outside and when she peeked out, she saw Tom. He was pacing back and forth beneath the window and he seemed highly agitated.

Without telling Cord what she intended, she ran back to the breezeway and outside and knelt beside the cat. His feet were wet and his coat was gnarled and covered with nettles and burrs.

"He's been in the swamp," she whispered. Her gaze moved out toward the moss-draped trees that stood like ghostly sentinels guarding the swamp.

The cat trotted away from her, then stopped and looked back.

"He knows where Hagan is," she said, her voice hushed with awe and disbelief.

"Sarah, that's crazy," Cord said indulgently. "Cats aren't like dogs. They don't lead us to people the way Rin Tin Tin did or—"

"Call it a hunch, like yours," she said, staring into his eyes. "But I know Tom knows where Hagan is. And I'm going to find him before it's too late."

"Oh, hell, no," Cord said. He glanced around cautiously. "There's no way I'm going to let you go off into that swamp by yourself."

Ignoring his protests, Sarah went back into the work-shop. She found a knapsack and began stuffing items in-side—bottled water, a flashlight and matches, canned food—things she kept in one place in case of an emer-gency.

"I grew up here. I know the swamp like I know the back of my hand."

"I don't care if you do," Cord growled. "This is crazy."

"I'm going. You can come with me, or not."

"Sarah, listen to me. I have to report this to the agency," he said. "This has gone too far and it's gotten too big for me to continue handling it on my own."

"Fine," she said. She sprayed her legs and clothes with insect repellent and stuffed it in one of the bag's pockets. "You do that. At least after I've found Hagan they can take him out of here."

"Sarah, there's no way I'm going to let you go. We have no reason to believe Hagan's out there, except for this stupid cat."

"Tom is not stupid."

"If I have to hog-tie you to keep you from doing this, I will."

As they stared stubbornly into each other's eyes, there was a loud explosion out near the road. Cord jumped and pushed Sarah back against the wall.

"Don't move," he said.

She was scared. She'd be lying if she said she wasn't. But she knew this was her chance. And she also knew, scared or not, that for Hagan's sake, she had to take it.

As soon as Cord left she hurried outside where Tom was still waiting. Then, keeping low and staying behind bushes and trees, she ran toward the swamp. Out near the main highway she heard the sputtering sound of an old log truck, and then a backfire and she smiled, relieved that Cord was safe at least.

"But he's going to be furious," she muttered as she ran.

Tom bounded through the tall grass, sometimes ahead of her, sometimes behind. Once he stopped and glanced back toward the house and Sarah knelt down in the tall grass. Then, seeing nothing through the swaying sawgrass, she hurried on toward the woods.

She pushed her way through Spanish moss and spiderwebs, scanning the ground for footprints. But if Hagan had come this way, he had been very careful. And the soft beds of pine needles were very good at masking footprints.

Still, Hagan was from the city, hardly used to this kind of life. And certainly not used to the danger of the swamp.

She was deep into the forest now and the ground was changing, turning into the soft quagmire, the "grassy waters" as the Indians once called it. Here, water glimmered everywhere, in small pools beneath trees, in the swaying grasses. It moved quietly beneath the grass, like a huge snake, shifting and turning, moving the grasses and lily pads as it passed.

Sarah had always loved the mystery of the swamp, but now she shivered, hoping she remembered the crooks and turns. Hoping that Hagan hadn't run headlong into this without thinking. Going into this area without direction could be deadly.

Tom didn't like it. He tiptoed around the water, shimmied up trees and arched his back every time he heard a noise. But he kept going.

Sarah's entire body was covered with sweat. The air was so still and hot that she felt as if she were in a sauna. It was getting late when finally she decided to stop and rest. She had to think.

She took crackers and a can of apple juice out of the knapsack and opened a tin of sausages for Tom. The juice was hot, but sweet and refreshing, and she drank it all.

She was just about to push herself up from the moss-covered ground when she heard a limb crack somewhere nearby. As she squinted through the shadowy trees, she noticed that Tom was looking in the same direction. When she stood up to get a better look, she saw him . . . coming through the underbrush.

"Hagan," she whispered. With a quiet, choked cry, she ran toward him, throwing herself against him and hearing his grunt of pleasure and surprise as she began to rain kisses against his hot skin.

"Good God, darlin'," he said, laughing.

"Oh, Hagan, I thought you were lost. I thought we'd never find you."

"We?" he asked, looking skeptically down at the cat as it rubbed against their legs.

"Tom led me here."

"No, I don't think so," he drawled.

"He did leave the house with you though, didn't he?"

"Well, yes, but I managed to make him go back."

"I knew it. That's why he knew where you were. Believe it or not, Hagan, he did lead me to you."

"Tom, the bloodhound," he said. Still, despite his sarcasm, Hagan bent down and rubbed Tom's fur. "You're a mess, cat. I have a feeling swamps are not your cup of tea, either."

Sarah couldn't seem to stop grinning.

"What makes you think that?" she asked.

"Old Tom and I, we're soul mates . . . remember?"

Her eyes sparkled as they looked into his. He was hot and sweaty and unshaven. His hair was tousled and wet, yet he looked vibrant, his eyes glittering with life.

"You...you look great, considering it's been less than a week since someone tried to kill you and only a few days since you were flat on your back, sick with a fever," she said, letting her surprised gaze wander over him.

"I am great," he said. "At least I'm doing *something,* even if it is running for my life. The question is, what in hell are you doing out here?"

"I came to find you."

"You mean you came to save me." He was deadly serious even though his eyes teased her.

"I...well...yes, I guess. I mean, you've never been in the swamps...you had nothing to eat and you—"

Hagan reached into his shirt pocket and produced a handful of blackberries. From his jeans pocket, he withdrew wild hickory nuts.

"Well...you certainly seem to have caught on in a hurry."

"Survival training. Deals with all kinds of terrain. But I am getting thirsty. Out here, I couldn't be sure what was rainwater and what wasn't."

"Here," she said, withdrawing her pack. She took out bottled water and handed it to him.

"God, you're a wonder," he said. As he drank the water, he kept his eyes on her. He reached out to touch her cheek and brush her damp hair back from her face.

"You all right?" he asked.

"I'm all right...now that I've found you," she added. "But I ran away from Cord. He's going to be very angry with me."

"Don't worry about Cord," he said. "Cord can take care of himself."

"That's exactly what he said about you."

"He did, did he?"

"We came home and found the house had been wrecked and I was scared out of my wits."

"I know, baby. I'm sorry about your house." He reached out and pulled her to him, holding her close for a moment, before looking down into her eyes.

"Hagan," she said, her voice hushed. "You've remembered your past, haven't you?"

"Yeah," he said quietly. "Most of it. Everything except what happened to Cindy the night the undercover went bad. Why... how did you know?"

"Just the way you talk about Cord. You sound more familiar when you say his name. And he thought he saw your initial on the windowsill in the workshop."

"So, he found it. Look, I'll tell you all about it later. Right now we need to move. Maybe find a little higher ground if you know anyplace like that. The men who broke into your house are not city boys like me. They'll know their way around this quagmire and once they decide to come looking here, we could have a problem keeping out of their way."

"I can do better than that," she said. "There's an old fishing cabin about a mile from here, although I can't vouch for the condition it's in."

"We'll worry about that when we get there," he said.

Sarah led the way. She could hear Hagan muttering quietly behind her as they moved through areas heavy with brush and briars. Tom was still with them and she could hear him grumbling, too. She glanced behind her, noting how the cat picked its way gingerly through the water and brush.

"You two are just alike," she said, smiling.

The darkness was slowing them down as Sarah took out her flashlight and waved it over trees and various landmarks. She was praying that she would be able to find the old shack in the darkness when she saw a shadow looming just ahead of them.

"There it is," she whispered.

"Turn off your light," Hagan said.

She did as he said and they waited for long minutes. They could hear the sound of egrets and herons as they settled in for the night, and somewhere in the distance came the roar of a bull alligator.

No matter how many times Sarah heard it, the sound still sent chills through her body. Native or not, she wasn't exactly crazy about being out in the swamp at night herself.

She felt Hagan's hand on her shoulder, squeezing reassuredly before nudging her forward again.

The shack was partially covered by trumpet vines and night creeper. And as Sarah stood letting the light move over the structure, she shivered.

"You're not cold?" Hagan said.

"I don't like this place," she said. "I never did."

"It looks pretty good to me. Anyplace out of the water and away from the mosquitoes. Why don't you like it?"

"Snakes," she said, shivering again.

"You don't like snakes?"

She could hear the teasing in his voice.

"My pretty little bayou queen doesn't like snakes?"

"Don't joke about this...I'm serious. I can't stand snakes. And don't pretend you like them any better than I do."

"Actually, I think they're pretty neat. Snakes are the least of our worries at the moment."

"You might not think they were so neat if you'd ever been out at night and had one slither over your bare foot." Sarah shuddered.

Hagan laughed softly.

"Come on, let's go in."

"Not until I've checked every inch of this roof and made sure one of those vines isn't a snake trying to fool me," she said.

Hagan laughed again and put his arm around her. He pulled her close against him and placed a kiss against her brow.

"I should be angry with you for doing this, you know," he said.

"I thought you needed me," she said. "How was I to know you'd turn out to be an Eagle Scout?"

"I do need you," he whispered.

Inside the shack, Sarah checked every inch of the place with her light before shrugging off her backpack onto a table that stood in the middle of the room.

"Oh, that feels good," she said, rubbing her neck and shoulders. She glanced at Hagan and smiled, then pulled some candles out of the bag.

"Please don't tell me we can't have light," she said, seeing the look in his eyes.

Hagan frowned. Every instinct in him wanted to say no, they couldn't risk lights. But seeing the fear on her face, he hadn't the heart.

"If we can cover the windows well enough," he said, searching around the one-room shack.

"Are you hungry?" she asked.

"Starving," he said, grinning at her over his shoulder. "You fix dinner, Jane, while Tarzan fix windows."

She couldn't help laughing when he grunted and slapped the palm of his hand against his chest.

Here they were hiding out in the swamp, possibly in danger of their lives. Having to spend the night in a squalid, bug-infested cabin where neither of them would be able to sleep a wink. And yet she thought his teasing and the sound of his voice was the most reassuring thing she'd ever heard. She didn't know how she could feel so happy, but she did.

Later, after a dinner of canned food and stale crackers, they sat on the floor on a rough army blanket, the same as the ones covering the windows. Even Tom had agreed to come inside for once and now he lay at their feet, curled into a ball, dry and purring with contentment.

Hagan had found a footstool and placed musty pillows against it, then covered them with blankets for a backrest. He pulled Sarah against him and they sat watching the flickering candles and listening to Tom's quiet breathing.

"Comfortable?" he asked.

"More than I'd have thought possible," she said, her eyes scanning the cabin suspiciously.

Hagan bent and kissed her mouth softly, then pulled away and gazed down into her sparkling eyes.

"When you and Cord left this morning, I found myself looking forward to one thing,"

"What?" she asked breathlessly, knowing perfectly well what his answer would be.

"Nighttime," he murmured. "And you. Cord would be gone and we'd be alone. I had hoped to make the most of what little time we had left."

"So did I," she said, smiling, even though the finality of his words hurt.

"Being hot and grimy and covered with bug bites is hardly conducive to making love, is it?"

Sarah laughed and hid her face against his chest. He smelled of sweat and swamp water and his shirt was still slightly damp.

"I'd settle for just being held through the night," she whispered.

"You've got it," he said, holding her tighter.

"Tell me about today," she said. "Tell me what happened and how you've remembered your past."

She lay cradled against him and she could hear the deep rumble of his voice as he spoke.

Hagan nodded toward the cat.

"Actually, Tom is the one who alerted me. Evidently he didn't take kindly to someone coming up onto his porch and waking him out of a sound sleep. He screamed like a holy terror. It's a wonder they didn't shoot him."

"Oh God, Hagan," Sarah said. "It scares me even hearing you talk about it."

"I was already in the workshop, climbing out the back window by the time I heard them crash through the front door. I could hear glass breaking, wood shattering. All the other tight spots I'd been in came back to me in a rush. Kind of like remembering a dream. Except I knew that what I was remembering was real."

He placed a soft kiss against Sarah's tousled hair. "I was torn between wanting to get out and wanting to save everything for you. All I could think about was what that place meant to you and how you would feel coming home to it after it was trashed. For one second, I almost didn't go."

"Oh, no," she protested. "I'm glad you did," she said, turning to face him. "Furniture and a house can be replaced," she whispered. "You can't."

Hagan shifted his weight and reached into his back pocket.

"I did manage to take one thing with me before I climbed out the window."

He pulled something out of his pocket and handed it to her, his eyes quiet and searching as he waited for her to take it from his fingers.

She sat up and spread the crumpled piece of canvas across her lap, staring at it silently for a long moment. It was one of the whimsical pictures she'd done of herself and Joe, holding a child she could only dream of and imagine on canvas.

"Oh," she whispered. "Hagan." When she looked up at him, there were tears glittering in her eyes. "This means so much to me. You have no idea."

"That's Joe, I take it?"

"Yes," she whispered.

"Why didn't you tell me there was a baby?" he asked, his voice soft with tenderness.

She wiped her eyes and stared down at the painting. It hardly even seemed real anymore.

"I wanted to. I would have," she said. "The doctors said the trauma of the accident and Joe's death caused the miscarriage. It was too early to know if it was a boy or a girl, but somehow I always imagined it was a little girl." She looked into Hagan's eyes and saw the tenderness and the understanding. "I was only a few weeks pregnant...." Her voice, ragged with emotion, caught, then stopped.

Hagan reached for her, pulling her and the canvas back into his arms.

"I'm sorry," he whispered against her hair. "God, baby, I'm so sorry." He held her for a long time, until she stopped crying.

"I feel guilty as hell, pulling you back into all these emotions that you've been trying to forget for the past year. Getting you involved in this stupid agency business. None of it seems very important after what you've been through."

"No," she said, wiping her eyes and looking up at him. "Don't you feel guilty about anything. And your work finding this Satilla group is very important. Even if Joe hadn't been involved in it, I'd think that."

"I'm going to find them," Hagan said. He took her face between his hands and looked steadily into her eyes. "I swear to you that no matter what happens, I'm going to find the men who killed your husband and left you with that scar and nothing else except pictures you can only imagine."

Sarah nodded. She didn't trust herself to speak. And as she moved back into his arms, she didn't trust herself to expect anything else but this.

Just the moment. And the night.

Chapter 14

Sarah woke sometime later, uncertain what time it was or how long she'd been asleep. The candles had long ago sputtered and died and there was a faint light rimming the edge of the blankets at the windows.

Hagan was still sleeping and she lay quietly against him, staring hard to see his profile in the dim light and listening to his quiet, steady breathing. Her back and neck felt stiff, but she didn't want to move and wake him.

She knew Tom was awake. She could hear him purring and when something soft rubbed against her hip, she jumped, then muttered softly.

"You silly cat. You scared me."

Hagan stirred and murmured something in his sleep. Then instantly he was awake, his hand going out to grasp her arm. She was also aware of him reaching for the gun that he'd laid on the table.

"It's all right," she whispered. "It's just Tom. I think

he wants to go outside. I'm surprised he's stayed indoors this long. Go back to sleep—I'll let him out.''

When she came back to the blanket, Hagan pulled her down beside him, flat on the floor now.

"God," he muttered, moving restlessly against the hard floor. "What I'd give for a shower and your nice soft bed." His voice was husky and soft with sleep. "The scent of roses in the air..."

His voice drifted off and Sarah smiled into the darkness.

Uncomfortable as it was lying on the rough blankets, she loved the feel of his body next to hers. She didn't know how she'd be able to manage to sleep alone again once his case was finished and he was gone.

"Don't think about it," she scolded herself.

"Hmm?"

"Nothing," she whispered, moving her hand to his chest. "Go back to sleep."

When they woke it was midmorning. The cabin was still dark because of the covered windows. But the summer sun was up and had turned the interior stifling hot. The air was very still, the kind of stillness that her grandfather always said preceded a storm.

They took turns going outside, and after they'd eaten a sparse breakfast, Hagan paced the floor restlessly.

"I need to get to Cord," he said. "Somehow I have to let him know where we are and find out what's going on."

"We could go back to the house."

"Too risky," he said. "They probably have someone watching your place." He stopped pacing for a moment and ran his hand down his unshaven face.

"I have a friend...Lacy. She could find Cord. I've known her since grade school. If I can't trust her, I can't trust anyone," Sarah said.

Hagan bit his lip and shook his head.

"No," he said. "I don't want to do that. Are there any service stations near your house? Anyplace where there might be a public telephone?"

"Not toward town," she said. "But to the north, out toward Millwood, there's a place. It's quite a hike, more than five miles from the house and even farther from here."

"How much food's left in the knapsack?" he asked, nodding toward her bag.

"Not much," she said. "A couple of cans of juice, the crackers, and maybe two cans of stew. I left too quickly to think about bringing money."

"It's all right. This will do for the day," he said thoughtfully. "If everything goes well, that's all we'll need. When it gets late, we'll start out of here, toward this place you're talking about. We'll use the pay phone to try to track down Cord."

"At least we won't need money for that. I know my phone card number," Sarah said.

"Good. We'll call after dark. If we're lucky, maybe by tomorrow you'll be back in your own house and your own bed." His eyes darkened as they moved over her features. The look of tiredness on her beautiful face tore guiltily at his heart.

Sarah ignored his remark and his look. How could she tell him that she would give up her comfortable bed, give up her grandparents' beloved house even, for more nights with him? She didn't care about the discomfort. All she cared about was being with him.

"Just before I left the house, Cord said he was thinking about calling the agency in on this. He said it was getting too big for him to handle alone," Sarah said.

"That's what he always says. But I know him—he's independent and he hates to admit defeat. He'll wait as long as he can about doing that. If he can get the proof on his own that the sheriff's involved, that's what he'll do."

Hagan came to Sarah and knelt beside her.

"Are you up for this hike tonight?" he asked. "You look a little pale."

"I'm all right," she said. "But I don't know what we'll do with Tom—it's too far for him."

"We'll have to lock him inside."

"Oh, Hagan . . ." she whispered, her eyes stricken. "I don't want to do that. You know how he hates being cooped up."

"It's for his own good," he said. "Sometimes cats like Tom have no idea what's good for them . . . or what they really need."

"Oh?" she asked. "And what do they really need?"

"A dry house and a warm bed to come home to," he murmured, moving closer. "Someone to love them."

"I told you, cats don't know about love," she said.

"Oh, but I think old Tom here knows," Hagan said with a slow, knowing smile.

"I . . . I thought you didn't believe in love," she whispered.

"I said I didn't know what love was," he said. "It's not something I've ever trusted in."

"But you trust me," she said, sliding her arms around his waist.

"More than anyone," he agreed. He wrapped his arms around her, feeling her soft breasts flatten against his stomach.

Hagan wanted her. He wanted to make love to her right here and now. Despite the filth of the cabin and despite their sweaty bodies and clothes.

But oddly, he found himself for the first time thinking of someone besides himself. His first concern was for her. He wanted to please her and to have their lovemaking be perfect, and he didn't want anything to tarnish that.

He could wait. If somehow he could just find a way out of this mess, he could wait. The way he was feeling at this moment, he thought the wait would definitely be worth it.

When this case was over, he had no idea what he was going to do about her. How he was going to leave. But he couldn't stay. In the back of his mind, he knew he couldn't risk putting her in danger again. And he wouldn't expose her to a life where she'd be constantly afraid for him or where she'd always have to live in fear that everything would be taken from her again.

Her life was calm and quiet. As sweet and wholesome as she was. How could he ever expect her to leave such a life for someone like him? A man whose everyday life involved the sleaze and filth of the criminal underworld.

He couldn't. When this was over, *everything* had to be over. That was the only way it could be. And he had a feeling Sarah knew that as well as he did.

"We'll leave before dark," he said, still holding her. "By this time tomorrow, it could all be over. And you can get on with your life, Sarah. And forget all this ever happened.

She held on to him as if he were her lifeline. She buried her face against his chest and closed her eyes. How can I forget it happened? she wanted to cry. Could he really expect her to forget him and all they'd shared so easily?

He pulled away and looked down at her.

"Let's go outside," he said. He found it hard to breathe when she was so close. When she looked up at him so trustingly with those deep blue eyes. "Someplace where we can at least see the sun."

Sarah's expression changed. Her eyes sparkled and for the first time in days there was a happy, carefree expression on her face.

"I know the exact spot," she said. "Here, you take the knapsack and I'll take one of these blankets." She wrinkled her nose as she shook out the blanket, then rolled it up and tucked it under her arm. "It's musty, but it's better than sitting on the ground."

"What are you up to?" he asked, loving the look of happiness on her face.

"You'll see."

They walked for more than a mile, with Tom following along behind, meowing to let them know he wasn't pleased with the day's outing at all. They pushed their way through brush, stopping now and then for Sarah to point out various things of interest to Hagan.

"This mushroom is actually very good for cooking," she said, brushing aside leaves and touching the large edible fungus. "Granddad and I used to go on hunting expeditions for these. Grandmother's mushroom sauce was the most wonderful thing you ever tasted."

Moments later, she stopped, placing her fingers against her lips to signal Hagan's attention and quiet.

It took a moment for his eyes to adjust to the shadows beneath the green undergrowth and to see what she and Tom were both staring at.

Across a small clearing was a doe with its fawn. The mother's head was lifted, eyes wide and ears pricked as she sensed their presence. But at her feet, the young deer continued to nuzzle beneath the ground cover in search of tender young grass sprouts.

Tom's back was arched as he stood perfectly still... waiting.

"Behave yourself, Tom," Hagan whispered.

Suddenly the doe nudged her baby and bounded away into the thicket, the fawn close at her heels.

"Weren't they beautiful?" Sarah asked, her eyes wide and filled with wonder.

"*You're* beautiful," Hagan said.

He loved her grace and compassion. And he loved the way she looked with the dappled sunlight across her nose. But most of all he thought he loved her heart and her goodness . . . her enthusiasm for the smallest, most simple things in life. It filled him with unexplained joy and hope. That was something that had been missing in his life as long as he could remember.

He kissed her, feeling his body respond as she opened her lips to him and moved tightly against him. The blanket dropped from her arms.

Hagan found his resolve weakening. And for the life of him he couldn't think of one single good reason why he shouldn't make love to her right then and there. Right on the soft pine needles and swamp moss at their feet.

Sarah laughed up at him, taking his hand and pulling him farther through the woods.

He grumbled a protest, but she only looked at him over her shoulder with a knowing look and a promise in her sparkling eyes.

When they stopped moments later, he understood.

It was the perfect place for lovers.

Hagan thought it looked as if it once had been cleared, but now the trumpet vines and ground cover crept over ancient stumps and fallen trees. Masses of huge green fern grew everywhere, enclosing the area as perfectly as if it had been landscaped for that purpose. But to Hagan the most surprising thing was an oval-shaped pool of onyx water that lay in the middle of the stand of moss-draped trees.

Shafts of sunlight filtered through the green leaves, making lacy patterns against the ground and water.

Sarah watched his face, noting the look of awe and surprise. Gently she tugged his hand, pointing out another pool at the side of the larger one. This one was smaller and lined with smooth, flat rocks. Although it blended perfectly with the natural setting, it was obvious that the mortared pieces of rock had been set by hand.

Hagan frowned and looked at Sarah.

"Whose land is this?"

"Ours," she said. "My family's I mean. Although I guess I'm the only one left to claim it now."

He shook his head and stepped to the edge of the smaller pool. He knelt down and let his fingers trail through the cool water.

"The water is clear," he said. "I always thought swamp water was black."

"The black color comes from the vegetation," she explained. "But the water is actually clear. It used to be some of the purest in the country, before developers moved in."

Sarah walked to the other side and began to clear pine needles from the bottom and push aside the vines that threatened to cover the pool.

"Granddad made this for me because he knew how scared I was of water moccasins. It's large enough for several people, kind of like a hot tub without the hot," she said, smiling. "But shallow enough to see the bottom so I wouldn't be afraid. The water from the larger pool flows through here in a filtered pipe, and out the other side. See," she said, pointing out the drains.

Hagan nodded and Sarah smiled at his look of disbelief.

"It hasn't been used in ages," she said.

Hagan looked across the pool into her eyes. He felt as if he were in some primeval forest. He had the whimsical vision of himself as an ancient Seminole chieftain and Sarah as his doe-eyed princess, just waiting for him to reach across the water and take her hand.

"Well?" she asked softly. "Would you like to try it?" She scratched in the vines and uncovered a large piece of white rock, holding it in her hand and offering it to him. "Soapstone . . . it's just like soap."

His answer was to stand up slowly and begin to unbutton his shirt. Still watching her eyes, he pulled his arms out of the sleeves, shrugging his shoulders and tossing the shirt onto the ground.

Tom, watching from a nearby tree, immediately pounced on the shirt, pawing it with leashed claws before flopping down onto it and stretching our lazily.

Hagan's naked chest gleamed in the dappled light that filtered through the dark canopy of trees. There was only the sound of trickling water and bird song in the forest.

For Sarah, the sight of him there in this most ancient of places was enough to take her breath away. He was different here. Not an agent nor a city man born and bred. But just a man, gloriously beautiful in all his masculinity. Perfectly formed, his skin dark and sleek, his eyes challenging and sure.

The way he looked at her made her heart skip crazily in her throat.

She had no words to describe how he made her feel. But in slow, hypnotic movements, she began to mirror his actions, unbuttoning her shirt and pushing it aside, standing across from him in her jeans and lacy bra. A light breeze played against her skin and fluttered wisps of hair around her face.

They had made love. He had seen her naked and vulnerable. Yet here in the daylight, in this surreal setting, it was completely different.

She thought he looked like a magnificent ancient king. Imposing and proud. Strong and ready to conquer and claim anything he wanted.

They both undressed and stepped into the pool at almost the same time, meeting in the center as Hagan reached out to take her hand and pull her against him.

Sarah gasped as their heated bodies met in the cool water. She could smell the water and the earthy scent of leaves and humus, mingled with the more intoxicating scent of his male body.

"Now," he said, his voice soft and husky. "Let's see how this works."

He took the soapstone from her fingers and, still looking at her, bent to dip it into the water. Without touching her anywhere else, he gently rubbed the milky stone against her neck and face and down along the fragile bones of her shoulders.

Sarah closed her eyes, giving in to the pleasure of the cool water and the pungent scent of the soapstone. She was completely under the spell of the moment.

Hagan's eyes took in every inch of her as he rubbed the soft, milky stone over her body. Without a word he turned her in his arms, dipping the stone in the water again as he pulled her back against him.

He shuddered when her naked hips touched his heated skin. At the same time, his hands moved around her to cup her breasts and gently wash them.

Hagan groaned and turned her again to face him, unable to resist the lure of her breasts and the sweet scent of her body.

"Hagan," she murmured, smiling and shaking her head against the passion that threatened to overwhelm both of them.

"Wait," she said. "Let me...return the favor." She took the stone from his fingers and bent to dip it into the water. Gently she reached out to touch it against Hagan's chest.

She washed his arms and chest. Then his throat, finally reaching up to his face and laughing softly when the residue turned his rough beard white.

As she continued to cleanse his skin with the soapstone, Hagan dipped his hands beneath the water, smiling when Sarah gasped and closed her eyes for a moment.

His fingers beneath the cool water felt hot as they moved over her body. Touching, caressing, enticing her until she thought she would die.

"Oh... my," she whispered. She forgot the soapstone, and let it drop from her fingers to leave a trail of white in the water.

Her whispered words caused Hagan to smile. He bent his head and kissed her, letting his mouth and tongue tease and tantalize just as his hands had. Playing a sweetly tortuous game with her and with himself.

Finally, as his hand and mouth grew more demanding, Sarah groaned and slid her arms around him.

She was so hot. Even the cooling water couldn't banish the heat that flooded over her.

"Enough..." she whispered.

Hagan laughed softly, then let his mouth trail along her scarred cheek, down her chin to the hollow of her neck. And lower.

Sarah's knees threatened to give way beneath her. Her hands dug into his shoulders even as she made a quiet sound of pleasure at the feel of his mouth against her breasts. His hands ran down her body, stopping at her hips and holding her still as he bent to trail teasing kisses over the curve of her stomach.

"Hagan..." she gasped.

When she thought she couldn't possibly stand another moment of his sweet torment, she felt him reach down and scoop her up in his arms. She tightened her arms around his neck as he stepped from the pool, then lay her on a soft bed of moss.

"You are a swamp witch," he whispered against her skin. "A beautiful, sexy swamp witch who's cast a spell over me."

"Tell me how," she said, moving against him, wanting him, her body pleading with him to take her.

"You make me forget everything," he said. "Everything except this..." His teeth nipped softly at her nipples. "And this..." he continued, moving up to kiss her mouth. "And you, Sarah. Always you. In my dreams. When I'm awake. Even when my head is telling me that this is insane."

Hagan slid his hands beneath her hips and she met him with an urgency that surprised even herself. She watched the play of emotion on his face as he took her. Saw his eyes spark, then grow languid when she cried out her pleasure.

There was something almost spiritual about making love there by the pool. With the scent of nature on their skin and the heat of their hot naked skin burning through the effects of the cool water.

The primitive setting brought a wildness and a recklessness to their lovemaking that even the danger couldn't have done.

Hagan's body was demanding. Driving both of them with a hard passion that blotted out everything around them. Sarah felt almost detached from her surroundings as she quickly felt her body responding to him and this overpowering eroticism. She met his hungry demands, growing liquid with sweet, hot passion. It sang through every inch of her body, moving her closer and closer to some distant place until she could no longer hold back her cries of passion.

"Sarah," he whispered against her skin, holding her, feeling her small body shudder. Until he found himself following her ascent out of control. "Oh . . . Sarah."

Later they lay for long moments, her legs still around him as they kissed and whispered their wonder and pleasure. Sarah lifted her mouth to his time and again, savoring the feel and scent of him. Letting her hands trail over his chest and shoulders as if she couldn't quite get enough of him.

"I've never experienced anything like this . . ." he whispered finally " . . . in my life."

"No," she said, making a weak protest. "A sophisticated man of the world like Hagan Cantrell . . . you're teasing me."

"I'm not teasing," he said. He raised himself up, propping himself on his elbow as he looked down at her. His fingers touched her face, and pushed her hair back from her flushed face.

"I never knew there was anyplace in the world like this," he said.

"You like it, then?" she asked, her voice almost shy.

He glanced around the clearing, letting his gaze take in the quiet serenity and beauty.

"More than I can tell you," he said.

"I'm glad," she said. "It used to be one of my favorite places when I was a girl." She snuggled against him, savoring the breeze that raked across their naked bodies. "After I was married . . . I never came back here much."

"I guess tastes change," he said.

"It wasn't that," she said, her voice growing soft and thoughtful. "Joe thought I should sell the place after my grandparents died. I refused. It was kind of a sore spot for us after that."

Hagan frowned slightly, watching the pain of remembrance in her eyes.

"One of the few disagreements we ever had, actually," she said.

"He didn't like it?"

"Oh, I guess he liked it okay," she said. "But Joe grew up in the swamp just like I did. Where for me the swamp was freedom and beauty, for him it only meant poverty and entrapment. He said he'd had enough of swamp living to do him a lifetime. He wanted more than that."

"He wanted the kind of life that money from the land could buy," Hagan said, nodding as if he understood.

"Yes, I guess," she said.

"I used to think money could cure everything, too," he said. He picked up a pine needle and trailed designs over her skin, smiling at her when she shivered and pushed his hand away.

"Did your mother have property?" she asked. "Something you could call yours?" Sarah had often wondered about his expensive clothes. Now that she knew him better she knew he wasn't pretentious or born to money.

"Hardly," he muttered.

Hagan rolled over onto his back, putting his hands behind his head and gazing up through the leaves at the bits of blue sky.

"I discovered a knack for sports when I was young," he explained. "There was a guy at the neighborhood boys' club who encouraged me. He practically forced me to finish high school, not an easy task when the streets are calling to you, believe me. Then he helped me get a scholarship to Georgia Tech. I worked and went to school, saved almost every penny I made. I made some good connections in school and later I used them." He shrugged his shoulders against the moss and he seemed completely lost in his memories. "I bought some worthless property, dirt cheap. Or at least everyone told me it was worthless When an ambitious developer came along and bought it, I made a bundle. More money than I'd ever had in my life. That was about the time I went to work for the agency. I reinvested the money and kept working."

"Oh," she said, smiling at him. "So that's how you could afford such fine clothes on an agent's salary?"

"Yeah." He nodded. "I guess that meant a lot to me because I never had anything before. The security of having money in the bank ... being able to buy anything I wanted ... wearing anything I wanted. I swore I'd never be poor again."

"Kind of like Scarlett," she teased softly.

He turned to look at her. His smile was sweet and warm. And the way he looked at her made her insides feel like soft honey.

"Kind of," he said.

"So," she said. "You would have sold this place, too, if you were me? I've been offered a fortune for it."

His eyes changed, growing soft as he gazed around the pool and clearing.

"Never in a million years," he said, his voice soft.

Sarah felt her heart leap and she couldn't explain the joy that washed over her.

"This is a one-of-a-kind place, darlin'," he said. "After it's gone, there won't be another."

"That's exactly the way I felt," she said, staring at him with a mixture of disbelief and pleasure.

"If I've learned one thing over the years it's that money can't save you," he said, his voice growing distant. "And it can't save your friends."

"Have you remembered about Cindy?" she asked, touching his chest softly.

"Only in my heart," he said, placing his hand over hers. "I'm afraid my head still hasn't cooperated."

They lay there quietly, holding each other and letting the beauty and safety of this place enfold them.

"Sarah," he said, not turning to look at her. "If anything happens to me, I want you to know—"

"Don't," she said, sitting up suddenly. She placed her hand over his mouth and looked down into his eyes. She thought she actually saw tears in his eyes. "Please, Hagan . . . don't even say such a thing."

He nodded, and pulled her hand away and kissed it, then held it against his chest.

"I never knew someone like you existed in this world, Sarah," he said. "I had no idea."

Chapter 15

Later they spread the blanket on the moss and lay in each other's arms. They slept. Woke and made love. Ate lunch and slept some more.

It was growing late and Hagan sensed that Sarah hated to leave on the trek to the service station as much as he did.

Tom had long ago bounded off into the forest and from time to time they heard the sound of another cat. Sarah looked into Hagan's eyes, her look one of surprise and anxiety.

"He's fighting again," she murmured. "That crazy cat is going to get himself killed."

"You know, I don't think he's fighting...exactly." He was grinning at her. "I saw another cat at the edge of the woods earlier while you were asleep. I'm pretty sure it was a female."

"Oh," she said. Then she smiled and fell into his arms. "How on earth did he manage to find a lover out here in the middle of nowhere?"

"The same question I've been asking about myself," Hagan teased.

"Oh . . . you."

"I hate to leave this place," Hagan said, glancing up at the trees.

"I know," she said. "So do I."

"When I'm back in Atlanta in that tall concrete-and-glass building, I'm going to think of this place," he said. "And you."

A small sob caught in Sarah's throat, but she managed a smile anyway.

"I'm glad," she said. "You know, you really should get out more often, Agent Cantrell."

He nodded, his look more serious now.

"You're right. Guess I've always been too busy working and making money, to see such places as this. But from now on, that's going to change." He turned to her, smiling impishly now and nodding toward the small pool. "Do you want to bathe first or shall I?"

"Why don't we bathe together?" she suggested.

"Uh-oh," he said. "There she is again . . . that little voodoo witch, beckoning me into the swamp again. I think I'm in trouble."

"Yep," she said, laughing as she pulled him toward the pool. "You definitely are, Agent Cantrell."

They had very little time back at the fishing shack before leaving to find a phone. It was a longer hike out to the road than Sarah thought. She was also weaker and more out of breath than she'd thought.

They hadn't had to lock Tom up inside because he hadn't come back with them. Sarah didn't know whether to be relieved or alarmed. Every time he left she figured she'd never see the rascal cat again. But this might be the time that fear actually became reality.

"Don't worry," Hagan said. "Tom will be fine. He'll probably be back at the cabin by the time we get there."

It was dark when they finally came out onto the main road. Sarah recognized the spot.

"We're very close," she said, nodding toward the north. "No more than a mile this way, I think."

It was heavenly being able to walk on dry, level pavement for a change.

"If we hear a car coming, we'll have to get back in the underbrush," Hagan warned.

"Right," she said. Sarah couldn't seem to catch her breath and she thought she was more hungry than she'd ever been in her life.

"Are you all right?" he asked.

"I'm fine," she said. "Just a little tired and out of breath."

Hagan murmured a soft protest but Sarah only kept walking.

"If you can do this after the ordeal you've been through, I can make it, too," she said.

Luckily the phone booth was on the side of the service station building where they managed to make their way to it without being seen. There were very few customers out here and none of them came around to use the phone.

After several minutes, when Cord didn't answer his phone, Hagan grew frustrated. Sarah could see the muscles in his unshaven jaw working.

"Come on, come on," he muttered, cursing softly into the phone.

Finally he hung up and raked his hand through his hair.

"What are we going to do?" she asked.

"I don't know. It could be late when he finally gets back to his room. Cord has been known to work night and day when he's on a case. The longer we stay here, the bigger chance we take of being caught."

"I can still call my friend," she offered. "Have her see if she can find him. Wayland is a small town and Cord is a stranger. Believe me, everyone has already made it their business to know where he is."

"I don't like the idea of getting anyone else involved in this," he said, shaking his head. "Not only for her protection, but for ours, too."

"Lacy is one of the most honest, trustworthy people I know. We've been friends since grade school. If I can't trust her, I can't trust anyone. Besides, I don't think we have a choice now, do we?" she asked.

"I could call the agency. They'd have a team down here in a matter of hours."

"Is that what you want to do?"

"Not really," he said. "I'd rather not. Besides, if Cord thought it was best, he'd already have done it."

He chewed at his lip, then nodded.

"I guess you're right. We don't have any choices left. Does this friend of yours know where the fishing shack is?"

"Yes, she was there as a kid almost as much as I was."

"Could she bring Cord there?" Hagan asked.

"Yes, I'm sure she could. There's an old partially abandoned road that comes in partway, so it will be much easier for them, coming in by car."

"Okay, then, let's do it," he said, motioning her toward the phone.

Sarah breathed a sigh of relief when she heard Lacy answer the phone almost immediately.

"Sarah, where on earth are you? I've been trying to call you but—"

"Lacy, I don't have time to talk much. Just listen, okay? I need you to do something for me. Something very important."

She heard Lacy speak to someone else, her voice muffled, her words indiscernible.

"Lacy?" Sarah asked, frowning. "Is your mother there with you?"

"No." Lacy's voice sounded breathless and now she lowered it to a whisper. "That's why I've been calling you so desperately. I've been dying to tell you . . ." Her voice trailed away and she laughed softly.

"Lace?"

"I've met someone, Sarah." She practically sighed when she said the words. "He's different. Not like anyone I've ever met before. I can't wait for you to meet him."

Sarah covered the phone with the palm of her hand and spoke to Hagan who stood watching with a worried look.

"She has a visitor."

"See if she can get rid of him," he said.

"Listen to me, Lace," Sarah said.

Hurriedly she told her what she wanted, saying only that she was in trouble and that she'd explain everything to her later.

"You can't tell this to anyone," Sarah warned. "Not even the guy who's there with you. Do you understand?"

"Yes, but—"

"I'm really sorry to do this, but you'll just have to get rid of him somehow. I'm sure when you explain things to him later, he'll understand."

"Yes . . . yes, I'm sure he will, too. All right . . ." Lacy seemed puzzled, but now there was a note of concern in her voice. As if she seemed to understand Sarah's words for the first time. "Just tell me what you want me to do."

Sarah described Cord.

"Yes, I know exactly who you mean," Lacy said. "Every woman in town has noticed him."

"I need you to find him and bring him out to the old fishing shack."

"The old—?"

"Don't repeat what I've said," Sarah warned.

"Oh, yes . . . sorry. All right."

"I hate to ask you to do this, but I'm sure Cord will explain everything to you on the way. All right, Lace? Can you do it as quickly as possible?"

"Of course I can," Lacy said, her voice determined. "I'll leave right now. Are you sure you're okay?"

Sarah glanced at Hagan and smiled.

"I'm fine. Talk to you when you get here."

She hung up the phone and walked into his arms.

"I still don't like this," Hagan said. "Especially since someone was there with her."

"It'll be okay," Sarah said, hugging him tightly. "Lacy likes to talk, but she can be as discreet as anyone when she needs to be."

"I'll take your word for it."

Sarah glanced around the corner, watching as a customer walked out of the store with a carton of soft drinks and a loaf of bread under his arm.

"Lord, what I wouldn't give for a simple slice of bread," she muttered.

Hagan laughed softly.

"As soon as this is over, we'll raid your freezer again. And this time I'll do the cooking."

The promise in his eyes sent shivers down Sarah's spine. But in the back of her mind, she didn't let it fool her. He was trying to make her feel better, trying to give her something to look forward to. When all along, both of them knew he'd be leaving long before there was time for grilling steaks.

She didn't answer, but took his hand as he pulled her with him toward the shadows and back into the forest. It was getting late and Sarah thought they probably wouldn't make it back to the shack before midnight.

It seemed to take hours to find their way back. The direction seemed unfamiliar to her and for a while she was afraid they might be lost, that they might wander in the swamps for hours and when Cord came he'd find no one there.

Just when she was ready to express her worries to Hagan, she saw the outline of the small building ahead of them.

Hagan held her back, waiting until he was sure it was safe to go inside.

Once they'd checked the interior and lit candles, Sarah stepped to the front door and peeked out into the gloom. She was hot and perspiring from the humidity and as she gazed toward the shadowy, airless forest, she saw lightning flickering in the south.

"Tom?" she called softly. "Here, kitty."

"He could be gone for days, baby," Hagan said. She felt him move up behind her, felt his hand at her waist and his chin resting on her hair. "Come on back inside."

"It's so hot," she whispered, turning to him. "I think it's going to storm."

"It is hot," he agreed. "I was just having fantasies about another quick dip in that pool your grandad built." His voice was soft and tender, filled with that teasing quality she liked so much.

"Wouldn't that be glorious?" she mused, leaning her head wearily against his chest.

"You sound beat," he said. "Here, let me open the last can of juice for you. Come here."

She watched as Hagan spread a blanket on the floor and made a comfortable spot for her. She heard the soft swoosh of the can opening as he turned to offer the juice to her.

She walked to him, never taking her eyes off his face. Had anyone ever looked at her with such sweet concern? Or was it just the heat? Had the long walk in the drenching humidity done something to her brain?

She took his hand and let him pull her down to the blanket. As he cradled her in his arms, he held the can of juice to her lips. When she pulled away, he bent his head and kissed her fruit-sweetened lips.

"Oh, Hagan," she whispered. "If all this has taught me anything, it's that we shouldn't waste a moment of our lives."

"Oh, my little swamp witch is getting philosophical on me," he teased.

She nudged him playfully with her elbow, but continued talking.

"It's made me realize that I've lost a year drowning in self pity," she said.

Hagan murmured a low protest, but she shook her head, indicating she wanted to continue.

"No, it's true," she said. "I kept this scar as a kind of badge of pity. A badge that prevented me from seeing anyone or doing anything."

"You needed the time, Sarah," he said.

"I know . . . I did. But it's time for me to get on with it now," she declared. "And as soon as this is all over, I'm going to have the plastic surgery."

Hagan hugged her and kissed her softly on the cheek.

"Good," he whispered. "I'm glad."

"It's hard for me to think this will really ever end sometimes," she said. "Tell me about how we'll be back at the house soon, taking a nice cool bath."

Hagan moved them both farther down on the blanket, propping them up on the pillows as he held her tightly against him and offered her more of the juice.

"I think . . ." His voice sounded so soothing against her ear, his words soft and alluring. And his arms made her feel more secure than she'd ever felt in her life. ". . . that very soon, we'll be back at your house. And while you take your nice cool bubble bath, I'll be in the kitchen cooking your dinner. The air conditioner will hum softly in the background. Candles flicker on the lacy tablecloth and in the air . . ."

"Yes?" she whispered. "Go on. Don't stop." Her voice sounded sleepy and soft with pleasure.

". . . in the air will be that wonderful, clean scent of roses that I like so much. From now on, whenever I smell roses, I'll think of you."

Tears filled her eyes, but she said nothing. She only held him tighter.

Hagan cleared his voice and continued, his words softer now and slower.

"There will be music in the background," he said. "Blues. You like blues?" He moved his head to look down at her and saw her smile and nod.

"It's my favorite. B.B. King," she murmured, her voice wistful and lost in dreams. "Etta James and Robert Cray."

He lifted his brows in a look of appreciation.

"I knew there was something about you I liked," he said.

"Tell me more," she whispered.

"The salad will be fresh and cold, the steaks crispy on the outside and juicy inside."

"Hmm."

"Hot potatoes, with lots of butter and sour cream. We'll worry about cholesterol some other time."

"And chives," she said. "From my herb garden."

"Definitely chives from your herb garden."

"Oh God," she whispered. "I'm drooling. You're killing me."

"Me, too," he laughed.

He continued talking for minutes until he noticed how quiet the cabin had become. Sarah's body against him was soft and relaxed and when he glanced down he saw that her lashes lay closed against her cheeks.

Hagan touched her face and hair, closing his eyes as he placed a kiss against her forehead and pulled her back into his arms.

He thought about all the times in his life when he had wished for something he couldn't quite name. That wistful longing feeling in the quietest part of his soul that left him restless and dissatisfied. Now he knew that this was what he'd been looking for. Someone like Sarah to hold and to love. She amazed and delighted him and he thought if he made love to her for a million years it wouldn't be enough.

He was torn between wanting Cord to come and not wanting him to. Because he knew that Cord's arrival would mean he'd have to leave Sarah and the serenity of this strange, beautiful place where she lived. He'd had a lot of regrets in his life, but none more torturing than the fact that he couldn't have this woman in his life forever.

His memory had practically all returned now. All except that terrible night when Cindy died and they left him on the side of the road to die.

He had remembered her, though. Her blond hair, cut straight and short, streaked with sunlight. The small, muscular body, tanned and kept in the peak of condition at the agency gym.

She was a funny girl. Bright and sweet. Sharp with the male agents when they did something that offended her sense of feminist pride. Sometimes tender and shy when she looked at Hagan a certain way.

"God," Hagan murmured, shifting his weight slightly on the hard floor.

She'd been like a kid sister, tagging along with him on every assignment she could get with him. Cord laughed about it. So had the rest of the agents.

But they'd liked Cindy and respected her. When it came right down to business, she had been a good cop, willing to make tough decisions and willing to carry them through.

With a little more experience she would have made as fine an agent as he'd ever known.

Had he been responsible for her death? Was there anything he could have done to save her?

He wanted to remember and he couldn't.

Hagan glanced down at Sarah, letting his gaze wander over her tousled auburn hair, down to her face that looked pale in the candlelight.

She'd been through so much. He didn't want to put her through anything else. She deserved happiness. She deserved a regular guy who could come home to her every night. A man who didn't carry a gun into the bedroom or wake up in the middle of the night with nightmares about his job or the sudden vision of someone dying.

She needed children to care for. She'd substituted old Tom so quickly for her lost dreams, although he didn't think she realized what she was doing.

When he'd found that picture of her husband and the baby, Hagan felt as if he'd been kicked in the gut. Suddenly he'd known the full measure of her grief. He'd felt it, saw it in every small stroke of her brush on the canvas. He'd felt guilty as hell and for the first time, he wished it had been another house he'd stumbled into that dark rainy night. Another person besides Sarah who had become involved in this mess.

She'd spoken just now about how it had changed her. How it made her not want to waste another minute of her life. The experience had changed him, too. But nothing . . . nothing in his life had ever affected him as much as these few days spent with her. In her simple life here near the swamps, she'd shown him more beauty, more joy than he ever thought existed. She was honest and good, yet filled with a passion that surprised and moved him. That even now made his body stir from wanting her.

But would it have been better if he'd never known her and involved her? Even if that meant never touching her or looking into those expressive blue eyes? Never making love to her?

"No," he groaned softly. He had to catch his breath for a moment as he looked down at her sleeping face.

"Yes," he said, forcing himself to be painfully honest. He cradled her tenderly against him, not afraid now that she was sleeping to let the true emotion in his eyes show.

"Better for you, darlin'," he muttered. "But not for me. Definitely not for me."

Chapter 16

Hagan hadn't intended to sleep. He wasn't sure what the sound was that woke him, but he was more alarmed that he had fallen asleep than he was by the noise.

It was storming. As he lay very still, he was aware of the flash of lightning around the blanketed windows and the sudden, violent crack of thunder. It jarred the earth and actually seemed to send the soft earth beneath the cabin into tremors.

But it hadn't been the storm that woke him. His instincts and experience told him that much. That and the hair at the back of his neck.

Carefully he moved Sarah out of his arms and leaned forward, blowing out the candles on the table. Then he sat quietly, waiting and letting his eyes become accustomed to the darkness.

Sarah roused. He could feel her stiffen beside him when she woke in the dark and he wasn't holding her.

"Hagan?" she said, reaching for him.

He took her hand, pulling it to his lips for a brief moment.

"Shh, I'm here, darlin'. Go back to sleep. I thought I heard something."

"Maybe it's Cord," she said, coming fully awake. She sat up beside him, pushing her sweat-dampened hair back from her face. "It has to be Cord, doesn't it?"

"Or Tom, back from his prowl," he said carefully, not wanting to scare her. "You stay put," he said. "I'll see." He touched her shoulder as he stood up, then crouching low, moved toward the windows.

Hagan stood to the side of the window, squinting so that he could see through the crack without moving the blanket. His hand moved automatically to rest on the gun and holster at his side.

Through the rain he saw a movement in the stand of moss-hung trees that surrounded the cabin. But the wind was blowing so fiercely that he couldn't be certain if what he saw was the flailing tree limbs, or something else.

Then in a flash of lightning, he saw a glint...a glimmer of light on something at the edge of the woods.

Hagan sucked in his breath and held it.

"Hagan?" he heard Sarah whisper.

"Shh."

In the next burst of lightning, he saw the man crouched in the rain beneath the trees.

It wasn't Cord.

As Hagan watched, the man moved forward in a low run. Everything happened so quickly that there was no time to warn Sarah. Hardly time to pull his weapon from the holster and turn to the door before the man was there.

Suddenly, with a loud crash, the door burst open.

In a split second Hagan was aware of the scent of rain and swamp water coming into the still air of the shack.

Aware in an odd, crazy way of the pleasant breeze, cooler now with the storm.

There were two of them. Two men, one behind the other, assault weapons raised as they burst through the door, then lowered as the barrels began to spurt fire.

"Sarah!" Hagan yelled as he threw himself toward the door.

He landed on the floor in front of them, rolling over and firing twice at the man in front. The man fell onto Hagan with a grunt and one last lifeless gasp of air.

His body trapped Hagan's arm and the pistol against the floor.

Suddenly everything seemed dreamlike. His actions and those of the man turning the rifle toward him seemed to be in slow motion as Hagan struggled to pull his arm and gun free.

The man at the door was coming toward Hagan, staggering awkwardly like a lumbering giant in the darkness.

Hagan knew he was going to die and oddly his last thought was one of anger. He couldn't save her. It was happening all over again.

"No! Sarah!" he screamed as he pulled his gun free and raised it. His voice was lost in the blast of gunfire, his eyes sightless in the fire and smoke.

Then he remembered it all. In one violent rush, he remembered . . . the look of trust in Cindy's eyes when she'd looked at him that last time. The determination on her face as she fought with the men who held them captive in the van.

Why had she fought? And, dammit, why hadn't he been able to somehow get free of the ties that held him?

In a matter of seconds, the man had jerked Cindy to her feet and struck her, then dragged her to the cargo door. Hagan had felt all the blood leave his body as he lunged forward on his knees in horror, calling out her name and seeing her pushed from the van.

He realized he was in the cabin now, not the van. And that suddenly the noise had stopped and he was still alive. It was only in that eerie silence that he realized some of the gunfire had come from outside the cabin.

He could hear his own ragged breathing as he dragged himself completely free of the lifeless body on top of him. The second man now lay sprawled on his back, partly outside the cabin, partly in.

Hagan pointed his gun once again toward the door.

"Hagan," a voice called. "Don't shoot . . . it's me . . . Cord."

Hagan felt every ounce of adrenaline rush from his body. Suddenly he was weak . . . shaking from his efforts, and from relief.

And just as suddenly he realized there were no other sounds coming from the cabin.

"Sarah?" he yelled, turning, scrambling, half crawling toward the table where the candles were.

He found her behind the table, curled up with her back and hips against the wall. Her body was limp and lifeless.

"No," he whispered. "No...please God, not Sarah. Not Sarah!"

He couldn't find the flashlight and as he fumbled with the candles, he swept them and the matches onto the floor.

He was aware of Cord beside him, murmuring reassurances. And he was aware of someone else, a young woman who rushed in and fell onto her knees beside Sarah's still body.

"Sarah," she cried. "Oh, God...this is all my fault. But I didn't know. Sweetie, please believe me, I didn't know."

Hagan didn't know what her words meant. And at the moment he didn't care. He scooped Sarah up into his arms. His stomach tightened when he felt the blood on her face and in her beautiful hair. And he closed his eyes and groaned.

"Hold on, darlin'," Hagan whispered, pushing his face against her neck. "Don't leave me now . . . do you hear? You can't leave me."

He couldn't see for the tears that suddenly flooded his eyes and choked his throat.

"Let me look at her," Cord said.

"There's no time," Hagan said, marching with her in his arms toward the door.

"There's a cut above her eye," Cord said, moving with Hagan. "Maybe she hasn't been shot. Maybe the blood is just from the cut."

"Where's the car?" Hagan asked. He hesitated at the door before going out into the pouring rain.

"About a half mile," Cord said. "You wait here . . . I'll see if I can drive closer . . ."

"No," Hagan said, stepping out into the rain. "There's no time."

Cord and Lacy stood inside the cabin for a brief second. They exchanged glances and Lacy placed her hands over her mouth to stifle her sobs. They watched helplessly as Hagan bent protectively, covering Sarah's face from the rain with his head and hands as he stumbled down the steps and out into the darkness.

"Is he crazy?" Lacy asked, her words breathless.

"Yeah," Cord said wearily. "I think maybe right now, he is."

Cord grabbed one of the blankets from the window. Then he and Lacy hurried out into the rain to catch up with Hagan.

When they finally got to the car, Cord drove while Hagan sat in the front seat cradling Sarah against him. Cord's gaze moved toward him time and again, but Hagan said nothing. He only sat holding her, rocking her. Sometimes whispering soft words against her hair.

Lacy, sitting in the back seat, couldn't seem to stop talking.

. "I'm so sorry," she said, her voice choked with tears. "When I met Dan Brennan I had no idea who, or what, he was. When Sarah called tonight I tried to get away without letting him know what was going on. But he seemed to know anyway. He said he wanted to help...that he was familiar with the swamp. He said he could bring food and dry clothes to you before I ever found Cord. I...I thought he only wanted to help...because of me. God. Cord thinks he introduced himself to me just so he could find Sarah...and you."

"He was the man who killed Cindy," Hagan said, his voice dead and lifeless.

Lacy didn't know the man who held her friend. And she could hardly believe that Sarah had kept this secret from her all this time. But she couldn't deny the connection that existed between them, either. Not after watching his tortured face and seeing the tender way he held Sarah so gently against him.

She thought she'd never seen such anguish on anyone's face.

"I didn't know...please believe me," she whispered before finally sinking back against the seat.

At the emergency room, they had to practically pry Sarah from Hagan's arms.

"I'm going with her," he said.

"Sir...you'll have to wait here," the nurse said. Her gaze took in the group's wet, bedraggled clothes and their mud-stained shoes.

"Lady..." Hagan said through gritted teeth. "I intend going with her—"

"Hagan," Cord said quietly. He caught Hagan's arm, feeling the tensed muscles and the way he jerked away from him.

"Let them do their job. They all know Sarah. This is her hospital. They care about her and they want to help her. But you have to let her go."

Hagan closed his eyes and hugged Sarah against him, his eyes bleak and filled with pain. Then he took a deep breath of air.

The nurse pushed the gurney closer beside him, looking at him now with a mixture of awe and curiosity.

"Please..." the nurse said. "Just until we can decide what her injuries are. Then we'll call you in. I promise," she added, her professional voice growing soft with sympathy.

Finally, gently, Hagan lay Sarah on the gurney. But he held her hand and walked with her to the large doors leading into the examining room. After she was gone, he stood there, shoulders slumped, clenching and unclenching his fists.

"Hey," Cord said, putting his hand on Hagan's shoulder. "Come and sit down. I'll get us some coffee..."

"I'll get it," Lacy said, hurrying toward the vending machines.

When Lacy brought the steaming cups back, Hagan took his and glanced up at her. It was the first time he'd even really looked at her and for a moment reality struck him and he felt guilty.

"Thanks," he said, attempting a smile. "Sarah talked about you a lot."

Tears filled Lacy's eyes and she sank into a chair beside Hagan.

"I would die before I'd do anything to hurt her," she whispered.

"Hey..." Hagan sat his cup of coffee on a table and reached to put his arm around the young woman's shoulders. "I know that. And Sarah knows it, too. You did your best," he said, shaking her gently for emphasis. "It's all we can do."

Lacy began to tell them everything that happened. Cord, who had already heard it, only nodded.

"She still had no idea who Dan Brennan was until she found me," Cord said.

"I had an odd feeling about him, though. When he seemed so enthusiastic about helping find Sarah, it just gave me a real funny feeling," Lacy said.

"Brennan and Walsh had to walk to the fishing shack. If Lacy hadn't found me so quickly and showed me the road into the swamp..." Cord shrugged and looked into Hagan's troubled eyes. He'd never seen his partner this way and it worried him.

Hagan nodded. "Thank you, Lacy," he said, his voice quieter...calmer now.

The nurse stepped out into the waiting room and looked toward them.

Hagan stood up, holding his breath as he stared at her.

"Are you...a relative?" she asked.

Hagan frowned and hesitated a moment.

"No," he said. "Just a friend."

He wanted to be more. In that one brief moment, he knew he wanted to be much more than a friend. He'd known it all along.

"Sarah's awake—you can see her now."

Hagan let the air out of his lungs in one loud burst of relief. He didn't even think to say anything to Cord and

Lacy. He just headed toward the door where the nurse was pointing.

She looked so small lying there in that narrow white bed. So fragile in the dim light with the machines bleeping softly behind her.

She reached out her hand and Hagan thought it was the most wonderful moment in his life.

He held on to her hand tightly, reaching out to brush the hair back from her pale face. There was a small white bandage above her eye.

Hagan touched it gently.

"Stitches?" he asked.

She nodded, smiling tremulously. "I'm going to look like a scarecrow, but at least it's on the same side as the other scar."

"I don't care," he whispered. He bent to kiss her pale lips. "I was afraid you'd been shot. As long as you're all right, I don't care what you look like."

"They think I have a mild concussion, too," she said. "In the darkness I must have fallen against the table or something. But all I could think about was you and when I woke up and you weren't here, I..." Sarah swallowed hard as a tear slid from the corner of her eye.

Hagan murmured softly and wiped the tear away.

"Don't cry for me, darlin'," he whispered. "I can't stand to see you cry. Besides, don't you know? I'm just like an old alley cat with nine lives." He grinned down at her, for a moment his old mischievous self.

Sarah laughed, then groaned as she reached up to touch her head.

"Ouch," she said.

Hagan pulled a chair up beside the bed and, still holding her hand, began to relate Lacy's story to her.

"Cord got the evidence he needed on Sheriff Metcalf, too," he said. "He's a secret member of the Satilla bunch. His job was to make sure they didn't have any resistance from law enforcement when they transported their guns across the county."

"And to give them any information he knew about outside agency activities," she said.

"Right."

"I knew it," she whispered. "Somehow I always knew he was involved."

"Dan Brennan made a play for Lacy just so he could get to you," Hagan said. "And to me."

"Poor Lacy," Sarah said, her eyes wide with sympathy. "I feel so guilty for involving her in this. And you, Hagan," she said. "God, you were almost killed because I insisted on calling her..."

"Shh. That's enough of that. It's over."

"I need to talk to her. I know it's killing her that she trusted someone like Dan Brennan. And that he used her." She looked up at Hagan. "Is he dead?"

"Yeah... so is Emmitt Walsh."

Hagan could see the concern in her eyes.

Wasn't it just like her to think more about her friend than she did herself? He guessed it was one of the reasons he loved her so much.

The thought came so naturally to Hagan's mind, but it stunned him nonetheless. He released Sarah's hand and moved back in the chair, his mouth working soundlessly as he stared at her.

"Hagan?" she asked, noting the look of mystery in his eyes. "What's wrong?"

He laughed and rubbed his hand over his stubbly chin. Then he stood up.

"Nothing's wrong," he said. "Actually, everything is pretty much right. For the first time in my life." He bent to place a quick kiss on her lips.

Sarah frowned. She didn't understand what he meant, or why there was such an odd look of excitement in his eyes.

"Where are you going?" she asked.

"There's something I have to do. You rest. I won't be gone long."

By the time he returned a couple of hours later, Sarah had been placed in a private room. When he came in, she was sitting up in bed, eating breakfast. Lacy was there in the room with her.

"Well," he murmured approvingly. "I like this sight. Hello Lacy. How's our patient?"

Lacy smiled knowingly, her eyes taking in every inch of Hagan as he moved toward them.

"She's doing great," she said. "The doctors say she can go home tomorrow." Lacy touched Sarah's arm and moved toward the door, passing Hagan with an openly curious look. "Well, I'll leave you two alone...so you can talk."

Sarah pushed her tray aside, her eyes burning with curiosity as she watched Hagan approach. He had showered and shaved and was wearing new jeans and a shirt.

He was leaving.

As she fought the wrench of pain in her heart, she knew that he had come to tell her he was going back to Atlanta. He'd come to say goodbye.

"I have something to tell you," he said, coming to the bed.

"I know," she whispered.

He sat in a chair beside her bed and reached for her hand. Holding her fingers between his hands, he pulled them against his mouth, gazing at her with a look that simply took Sarah's breath away.

Sarah didn't want to cry. Didn't want to throw herself at him and plead with him not to go. But that was exactly what her heart was urging her to do.

"Say it," she said. "Just go ahead and say it."

Hagan cocked his head to one side and looked at her curiously. He tightened his grip on her hand and sat up straighter in the chair.

"In all my life, I've never met anyone like you, Sarah," he said. "I grew up pretty much on my own. With no encouragement, no kind words or expression of affection. And I told myself all this time that it didn't matter. That I, Hagan Cantrell, could make it on my own, with no help from anyone else."

"And you have," she said. "You've made a good life for yourself, Hagan. You should be proud."

"No," he said, shaking his head. His smile was sweet and a little sad. "Substitutions were all I ever had. I never really knew what life was supposed to be like. Cord and Georgia showed me a part of it, but I was still an outsider...still just an observer." He laughed softly and shook his head. "God, why is this so hard?" he muttered.

"Saying goodbye is always hard," she offered, her voice soft with regret.

"Goodbye? Oh, but, darlin', this is not goodbye," he said warmly. Then he frowned. "That's not what you want, is it? Goodbye? Not that I could blame you if you never wanted to see me again after—"

"No," she said quickly. "Heavens, no. Of course I don't want to say goodbye, but—"

"Lord, you thought...?" Hagan stared hard at her. "You thought I was going to leave? Just like that? Pick up and go as if nothing ever happened between us?"

"I—"

"I came here to tell you that I lov... that I lov..." Hagan laughed softly and bent his head until his forehead touched hers.

Sarah's eyes grew wide with awe and joy as she finally realized what he was trying to say. Her hand crept up around his neck and she trailed little kisses across his face and breathed in the clean masculine scent of him.

"Is it so hard to say?" she whispered against his ear.

Hagan's laughter was muffled against her skin before he pulled away and looked into her eyes.

"It's just that... I've never said these words to anyone," he whispered.

"Well, if you don't say them pretty soon, I think I'm going to just explode," she teased.

He laughed, then grew serious.

"I love you, Sarah James," he whispered, his voice husky with emotion. "God, I've never loved anything as much as I love you."

"Oh, and I love you," she whispered.

His kiss was sweet and warm, filled with all the tumultuous emotions that had followed their entire relationship. Yet today, with all that had happened and the realization of all that could have happened, there was a reverence and a gentleness that he had never felt for anyone.

He took her hands, leaning close.

"I've resigned from the G.B.I.," he said.

"You've...? Oh, no... Hagan," she protested. "You love your work. You're so committed and intelligent... so good at what you do."

"I didn't say I was getting out of law enforcement altogether," he said. "You do realize there will be a sheriff's vacancy coming up soon in Ware County, don't you?''

"Oh, my gosh," she whispered, her eyes sparkling. "Hagan Cantrell, Sheriff of Ware County. It sounds good." She frowned again. "But you aren't doing this... quitting the agency... because of me?''

"Partly," he admitted. "I want to be with you every day, Sarah. Not just once a week or on weekends, or calling from someplace in God-knows-where, Georgia. When dark comes, there's only one place I want to be—at home in bed with you."

"Oh..." Her eyes twinkled and her voice was one long sigh of pleasure.

"But I want it for me, too," he continued. "I've learned so much from you, Sarah. And I want different things than I wanted before."

"What things?" she asked with solemn awe.

"A home. Not just a designer-decorated apartment in the best part of town. But a real home, like your grandparents had. Land to pass on to my children and then their children. A place for them to grow up where everyone in town will come to their wedding."

Sarah's lips were parted as she stared at him in disbelief.

"I want you," he said. "Because you're real and caring... because I can talk to you about anything. And because you have such compassion for other people. I love you."

She held her breath, staring at him with eyes swimming in tears.

"Will you—?" he began.

"Yes," she whispered, reaching for him and stopping his words with a kiss. "Oh, yes."

Neither of them could seem to stop smiling. When a nurse stepped into the room, they pulled apart, grinning.

"Oh," she said. "I came in because we noticed a change in your heart rate and blood pressure on the monitor," she said. "But I'd say that's normal...under the circumstances."

"Nancy," Sarah said. "I'm engaged." Then she grinned at Hagan. "I am, aren't I?"

"You are," he said. "But not for long. We're getting married as soon as you get out of this place."

"Sarah, that's wonderful," the nurse said. "Here, I'm going to just unplug the heart and BP monitor. You don't need it anymore anyway. It would be kind of like voyeurism to keep watching, wouldn't it?"

They all laughed and when the nurse left, Hagan reached into his pocket.

"The strangest thing happened," he said. "When I went to buy the ring, I knew I could afford practically anything I wanted. But then I realized, looking at all those huge, ostentatious stones, that none of them would be what you wanted."

He slipped the ring onto her finger as she gazed up at him. It was a small cluster ring of diamonds and brilliant blue aquamarine.

"I thought they matched your eyes," he said.

"It's beautiful," she whispered. "Oh, Hagan I love it. And I love you."

Hagan climbed onto the bed with her, wrapped his arms around her and held her quietly for a moment.

"By the way, you might be interested to know that when I went back to your house to shower and change, Tom was back."

Sarah turned to look at him, her face glowing with life and love.

"He was? Oh . . . I was afraid this time he was gone for good."

"Darlin', old Tom knows a good thing when he sees it," he whispered. "He's not about to leave you . . . not ever. He's too much like me, remember? He did, however, bring a lady friend with him and they seemed quite cozy there on the front porch. I have a feeling Tom will be the one to contribute to our family first."

Sarah laughed and clapped her hands, then sat up in bed.

"You know what?" she said. "I think I'm ready to go home. I want to meet this lady friend of Tom's."

"Jealous?" he teased.

"No," she whispered against his lips. "Happy. Happier than I've ever been. I just can't wait to get started on our new life."

"Neither can I, darlin'. Neither can I."

* * * * *

COMING NEXT MONTH

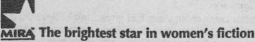

This July, watch for the delivery of...

An exciting new miniseries that appears in a different Silhouette series each month. It's about love, marriage—and Daddy's unexpected need for a baby carriage!

Daddy Knows Last unites five of your favorite authors as they weave five connected stories about baby fever in New Hope, Texas.

- **THE BABY NOTION** by Dixie Browning
  (SD#1011, 7/96)

- **BABY IN A BASKET** by Helen R. Myers
  (SR#1169, 8/96)

- **MARRIED...WITH TWINS!**
  by Jennifer Mikels
  (SSE#1054, 9/96)

- **HOW TO HOOK A HUSBAND (AND A BABY)**
  by Carolyn Zane
  (YT#29, 10/96)

- **DISCOVERED: DADDY** by Marilyn Pappano
  (IM#746, 11/96)

Daddy Knows Last arrives in July...only from

SILHOUETTE... Where Passion Lives

Add these Silhouette favorites to your collection today!
Now you can receive a discount by ordering two or more titles!

SD#05819	WILD MIDNIGHT by Ann Major	$2.99	☐
SD#05878	THE UNFORGIVING BRIDE	$2.99 U.S.	☐
	by Joan Johnston	$3.50 CAN.	☐
IM#07568	MIRANDA'S VIKING by Maggie Shayne	$3.50	☐
SSE#09896	SWEETBRIAR SUMMIT	$3.50 U.S.	☐
	by Christine Rimmer	$3.99 CAN.	☐
SSE#09944	A ROSE AND A WEDDING VOW	$3.75 U.S.	☐
	by Andrea Edwards	$4.25 CAN.	☐
SR#19002	A FATHER'S PROMISE	$2.75	☐
	by Helen R. Myers		

(limited quantities available on certain titles)

TOTAL AMOUNT	$_____
DEDUCT: 10% DISCOUNT FOR 2+ BOOKS	$_____
POSTAGE & HANDLING	$_____
($1.00 for one book, 50¢ for each additional)	
APPLICABLE TAXES**	$_____
TOTAL PAYABLE	$_____
(check or money order—please do not send cash)	

To order, send the completed form with your name, address, zip or postal code, along with a check or money order for the total above, payable to Silhouette Books, to: **In the U.S.:** 3010 Walden Avenue, P.O. Box 9077, Buffalo, NY 14269-9077; **In Canada:** P.O. Box 636, Fort Erie, Ontario, L2A 5X3.

Name:_____

Address:_____City:_____

State/Prov.:_____ Zip/Postal Code:_____

**New York residents remit applicable sales taxes.
Canadian residents remit applicable GST and provincial taxes.

Silhouette®

SBACK-JA2